KID SOLDIER

D1560145

KID SOLDIER

JENNIFER MARUNO

DUNDURN
TORONTO

Editor: Jennifer McKnight
Design: Jesse Hooper
Printer: Webcom

Library and Archives Canada Cataloguing in Publication

Maruno, Jennifer, 1950-
Kid soldier / Jennifer Maruno.

Issued also in electronic formats.
ISBN 978-1-4597-0677-4

I. Title.

PS8626.A785K54 2013   jC813'.6   C2012-908607-X

1   2   3   4   5   17   16   15   14   13

We acknowledge the support of the **Canada Council for the Arts** and the **Ontario Arts Council** for our publishing program. We also acknowledge the financial support of the **Government of Canada** through the **Canada Book Fund** and **Livres Canada Books**, and the **Government of Ontario** through the **Ontario Book Publishing Tax Credit** and the **Ontario Media Development Corporation**.

Care has been taken to trace the ownership of copyright material used in this book. The author and the publisher welcome any information enabling them to rectify any references or credits in subsequent editions.

J. Kirk Howard, President

Printed and bound in Canada.

VISIT US AT
Dundurn.com | Pinterest.com/Dundurnpress | @dundurnpress | Facebook.com/dundurnpress

Dundurn	Gazelle Book Services Limited	Dundurn
3 Church Street, Suite 500	White Cross Mills	2250 Military Road
Toronto, Ontario, Canada	High Town, Lancaster, England	Tonawanda, NY
M5E 1M2	L41 4XS	U.S.A. 14150

Dedicated to Richard Charles Fuller

CHAPTER 1

Spring 1939

The only fruit tree on a street of maples, the cherry tree towered above the privet hedge that framed the Fuller front lawn. In the spring papery blossoms dusted the yard like a layer of unexpected snow bringing fragrance to the entire neighbourhood. In the summer clusters of crimson heart-shaped fruit dangled from every branch and a thick canopy of leaves camouflaged a platform of planks. This huge tree, older than its two-storey wooden house, was a perfect place to watch the world go by.

"I'm going to look for a job this afternoon," Richard announced as he swung himself up to the floor of planks salvaged from Mr. Black's garage teardown.

"You're too young to get a job," Tommy replied, furrowing his brow.

In September Richard Fuller would turn fifteen the very day Tommy McLaughlin would turn ten. Despite the difference in their ages, Richard treated the boy with curly copper hair as his equal. If he had an apple, he cut it with his pocket knife and presented half, without Tommy having to ask. He had even made them a checkerboard for the tree house.

"What difference does a couple of months make?" Richard said as they began a game of checkers. "I'll be fifteen on our birthday." Richard's eyes, the colour of a summer sky, always looked as if he was about to tell a funny story. He shoved the shock of straight blond hair away from his eyes and grinned at the boy sitting cross-legged behind the stack of red and black bottle caps they used for checkers

"My dad says there's no work for anyone, anywhere, so no point looking," Tommy said, as he placed a Coke cap on a red crayoned square.

Richard didn't have a dad to give him direction or advice. He knew Tommy didn't want him working because he wanted to have fun with Richard over the summer. If it hadn't been for Richard, Tommy would have never seen the salvage operation that used dynamite to break up the Honeymoon Bridge. In January, Richard had taken Tommy to the gorge every weekend to see the collapsed structure lying on the ice below. All the onlookers gasped at the monstrous splashes that swallowed the last of the twisted metal as the ice cracked under its weight.

"Wanna tour the farms with me?" Richard asked.

"Sure," Tommy said, scrambling to his feet. "Maybe we'll see something in the river."

"What about Amy?" Richard asked.

"Third Saturday of the month," Tommy replied, landing with a thud, "and no maid."

Richard had forgotten about Mrs. McLaughlin's Saturday afternoon tea parties. Without a maid, Tommy's sister would have to push the heavy waxing machine across the hardwood floors before she polished the silver teapot and matching cream and sugar. By now, she would be setting out floral china cups for the ladies who left cards in the silver bowl on the hall table.

Tommy zipped up his cardigan and hopped on his bike. Richard walked coatless alongside him in the fresh air. The boys followed the road along the river.

On one side the cold, dark green water rushed from the falls to the whirlpool. On the other, the sweet oasis of orchards was alive with birdsong. Richard loved the sight of the jet-black tree trunks after a night of river mist.

"Some farmer's burning rubbish," Richard said when the air brought them the smell of smoke. It was also tangy with the smell of manure. All of it felt good to his nostrils.

They started with the Mason farm where the acres of short stubby trees began.

"All I gotta make is fifty-two dollars," Richard said as they made their way down the rutted lane. "Two cents a pint for raspberries, two cents a quart for strawberries, and five cents a basket for peaches," he rhymed off. "It'll take no time at all."

"Fifty-two dollars," Tommy repeated in amazement, circling him on his bike. That was a lot of money, in his opinion. "Why do you need fifty-two dollars?"

"For fifty-two dollars I can get what's in the front window of Cupola's Bike Shop."

Tommy went quiet. He had gotten his bike for Christmas, one of the advantages of coming from a family with a well-paid father. Although they lived in the same neighbourhood, Tommy dined at a walnut suite with cushion-backed chairs. Richard ate at a metal table with cracked vinyl seats.

Mr. Mason put Richard's name down for picking cherries. He told Richard they would get in touch when needed. Not having a phone, Richard left his neighbour's telephone number. He knew Mr. Black wouldn't mind.

The two boys walked Tommy's bike towards the next farm. A rusty red metal gate held a wooden plank sign with the dark letters, VOGEL, burnt into the wood.

Tommy dropped his bike to the ground. "You're not going to look for work with Old Man Vogel?" he asked.

"Why not?"

"That guy is crazy," Tommy whispered, as he pointed towards the old farmhouse with a peeling wooden verandah. At one time it had been dark green, but hadn't seen a coat of fresh paint in years. Twisted grey brush grew up through the porch's broken railing.

"Where did you hear that?" Richard asked.

"I overheard Jimmy Côté telling my dad," Tommy said. "He said Vogel took one look at the bushel of peaches he just picked and his eyes filled with tears."

Tommy looked up at Richard, but Richard ignored his over-big pleading eyes. He ruffled Tommy's tight curls. "You worry too much," he said. But Tommy knew Richard wouldn't have any trouble getting hired. Everything came easy for him. He climbed trees without having to figure out where his hands and feet went. He carved a horse the very day his mother gave him his father's pocket knife. In his corduroy pants, checkered shirt, and leather work boots, Richard already looked like a farm hand.

The snort of a horse and rumble of wagon wheels coming towards them caught their attention. The driver, in a pair of dusty overalls over a shabby sweater, had his face in the shadow of an ancient straw hat.

Richard rushed to the gate and swung it open. The man gave him a nod as the thick-planked wagon passed through. Richard closed the gate with a click. The man glanced back as he drove his horses out onto the road but didn't speak.

Tommy breathed a great sigh of relief.

They headed to the next farm along the road that rolled through the fruit trees. Both were surprised to find Vogel's horse and wagon waiting in the bend.

"You looking for work?" the man asked Richard in a surprisingly soft voice.

"Yes sir," Richard replied, straightening his shirt. He brushed back the strands of straight blond hair falling over his right eye, then turned to Tommy and grinned.

Tommy dropped his bike and walked to the front of the horse. "He came for a fruit picking job," he said in a very loud voice. "There's no fruit to pick yet."

The old man with the grey, grizzled beard studied Tommy for a moment, and then turned his watery blue eyes back to Richard. "Yes or no?" he asked.

"Yes sir," Richard replied.

"You want work now?"

"Yes sir," Richard repeated.

The old man tapped the seat of the buckboard wagon.

"You want to come?" Richard asked Tommy as he climbed up onto the wagon seat. The man's old woolen sweater smelled like his horse.

Tommy shook his head. He hopped on his bike and rode away.

Richard had only asked out of politeness. He knew Tommy would be in trouble if he was late for dinner. But Richard had all the time in the world. His mother never worried about him being late. She often fell asleep in her chair having no idea what time he got home.

CHAPTER 2

Mr. Vogel

Richard watched the wide back of the farm horse sway as it plodded along the river road. The old farmer's head nodded until his chin rested on his chest. The reins fell out of his hands, but Richard didn't try to take them. He figured this horse knew its way, even in the snow.

He put his hands behind his head and leaned back to watch the scenery go by. They passed a field of men stringing wire between posts to make a fence. Seeing the horse and cart, they raised their hands in salute. Richard waved back.

The orchards gave way to the wide green lawns of brick houses set well back from the road. Soon they passed small wooden houses, close to the road without any lawn at all. Mr. Vogel lifted his head when the horse slowed at the village intersection. He eased the beast around the corner and down the hill to the Queenston dock.

Richard gave out a long low whistle when he saw the huge ship with a black and white hull looming before them. He stared up at the broad white band that circled the stack, with a large black W painted across.

"I have to pick up special baskets," Mr. Vogel explained as the horse clopped on to the wooden dock. "My crop goes to the Toronto market, not the cannery."

Richard loaded the shipment of wide-handled, narrow wooden baskets on to the wagon. Later he unloaded them into Vogel's wooden barn at the back of the farm. The sun was almost gone from the sky by the time he finished.

Dusk softened the edges of the hedge when the horse and cart pulled up in front of the Fuller's dilapidated wooden house on Maple Street. Mr. Vogel handed Richard a quarter. "After school," he said in a low growl. "Tomorrow."

"Thanks," Richard said, leaping on to the sidewalk. "See you then."

———◆———

The house was hot and moist from his mother's full day of laundry. The smell of stew drifting through the scent of freshly ironed linen made Richard's stomach rumble. He hadn't eaten since breakfast.

"You're home," Grace Fuller said, making it a state-ment rather than a welcome. Tall and slim, like her son, she wore her hair in a single ponytail pulled to the nape of her neck. It was once all the shades of blonde there could be, but had faded to the colour of the dirty water she emptied from her laundry tubs. She remained behind her ironing board on a threadbare carpet in a room supposed to be for dining, but dedicated entirely to laundry. A faded flannel sheet covered half of the walnut table. On it sat the sewing machine she used for making small repairs. The other end held stacks of crisp linen and snowy towels.

The eight dining chairs, except for the one his mother sat in while sewing, had found their way to other parts of the house. The china cabinet that used be in the corner had sold long ago.

Grace Fuller never smiled and she had none of the prettiness of Tommy's mother. Once Richard had heard Tommy's parents talking about his mother in their garden. "She stopped smiling the day her husband died," Mr. McLaughlin said with a deep sigh.

Mrs. McLaughlin gave her dark curls a toss and raised her eyes to the clouds. "She spent little enough time smiling while he was alive," was her acid reply.

Richard knew his mother didn't have time for smiling, having had to support the two of them. She had tried working in the canning factory on Thorold Stone Road, shortly after his father's death, but she used all that she made on bus fare and babysitting. She had decided instead to take in towels and bed linen from the local hotels, along with other people's washing, for a living.

"I just got myself a job," Richard told her, flipping the silver coin in the air.

"Won't last long," his mother replied. Her iron came down with a thud on top of an embroidered hotel crest. "There aren't enough jobs for grown men."

"It will help pay for school books and a few clothes," Richard said. He didn't mention the bike in Cupola's window.

"Can't stop you from trying to earn," his mother replied with a grimace. She didn't even ask if he was hungry, just cocked her head in the direction of the kitchen. "Stew's in the pot," she said as she carried on ironing.

The next day, Mr. Vogel put Richard to work pulling weeds in the asparagus patch. On Saturday, he hoed around the base of the fruit trees.

"It wasn't a hard job," he told Tommy after dinner in the tree house. "But it was dirty. By lunch time I was caked with dust to the knees."

"Good thing your mother does washing," Tommy commented. "My mother would not have been happy about that."

"Mr. Vogel is a really nice guy," Richard said. "He tells me what to do and then leaves me to get on with it." *When Mr. Vogel does talk*, Richard thought, *he tells me stories about living on his family farm*. But, for some reason, he didn't share that with Tommy. Richard got the feeling right from the very beginning that Mr. Vogel, like his mother, was a very private person and didn't like people knowing a lot about him.

When all the hoeing and weeding was finished, slender green stalks of asparagus began to appear. Richard loved the sound of asparagus when he snapped a stalk from the ground. Having never tasted asparagus, Richard asked. "What do people do with this stuff?"

Mr. Vogel looked at him in surprise. "They eat it."

"I know that," Richard said with a smile. "But how?"

"Take a bundle home," the farmer said. "Your mother will know."

Mr. Vogel set Richard to work in the barn. He graded asparagus according to size, while Mr. Vogel filled the baskets.

Richard's first packing job was to cover the baskets of asparagus with leno, an orange mesh that kept away the flies. Then he was to stamp the wooden handles with the words "Vogel Farms" in black ink. Richard took extra care to make sure he didn't smudge the letters.

Mr. Vogel nodded in approval.

Friday night they loaded the baskets of asparagus onto the wagon and took them to the steamer waiting at the Queenston dock. The ship crossed Lake Ontario at night to arrive in time for the morning market in Toronto.

"Have you ever been on a steamer?" Richard asked when the wagon was empty. He couldn't stop thinking about living in one of the small cabins he could see on deck.

The old man nodded and stroked the front of his grizzled beard. "Arrived at the Port of Toronto on one of those," he said.

"It must be great to sail off to new places and see new things," Richard said. He turned to the old man at his side. "One of these days," he announced, "I'm going to get on a steamer like that and see the world."

The two of them sat in the wagon watching the ship move away from the dock.

"Where did you come from?" Richard asked.

Mr. Vogel stared off into space for so long Richard figured he wasn't going to answer. Then he jiggled the reins and spoke in low tones, just above the clopping of the horse's hooves.

"My story began in Holland," the old man said. "After the war of 1914, my brothers and I returned to a destroyed farm. Our parents could barely feed themselves."

He stopped speaking when the horse entered the intersection, and then began again.

"The three of us found work on a cattle boat and left to find our fortune. We landed in Toronto, paying room and board while we worked at the Kensington Market. After a few years, Paul, my youngest brother, had saved enough to buy a vegetable stall. Mark and I decided to buy some ground and grow for his business. That's when we bought this farm."

It wasn't until they returned to the barn that Mr. Vogel continued his story.

"We lived in the barn until we built the house. But farming was too hard for Mark. He died one day of a heart attack in the middle of the orchard."

Richard remained silent the whole time. He knew Mr. Vogel had probably told him more than he'd told anyone else in the world.

CHAPTER 3

Mr. Black

When school finished Richard spent full days at the Vogel farm. He ate his lunch on the wooden bench next to the shed behind the barn. Other than the trees in the orchard the barn provided the only shade.

"What do you keep in there?" he asked one day, jerking his head in the direction of the small outbuilding.

Mr. Vogel reached for a key that lay on top of the door frame. He tossed it to Richard and went back into the barn.

Richard unlocked the door's padlock and stepped into the dim interior. It took a few minutes for his eyes to adjust from the bright sunlight. At first all he could see were a few ancient bales of hay and a couple of lidded wooden crates. Then a large object under a canvas tarpaulin came into view. He peeled back the tarp. The tractor, not much bigger than a young fruit tree, was the colour of a raincloud. Richard ran his hand across the nose, removing a swath of dust. A small plate read CASE. His heart soared at the sight of such a famous brand.

"Where did you get it?" Richard shouted out.

Mr. Vogel entered the shed, dragged one of the bales of hay next to another, and pointed for Richard to use it as a seat. He removed his hat and ran his fingers through his grey-flecked hair. "My brother bought it from another farmer because it needed fixing. I told him it would probably cost more to fix than he thought, but he brought it into the shed." He shook his head. "Shortly after he died, those crates arrived."

"And you never opened them?" Richard looked at the old man. "You're going to let that tractor sit and rust while you could be using it to plough the fields?" He raised his eyebrows in disbelief.

Vogel shrugged his shoulders and put his straw hat back on his head. "Gasoline costs money," he said, rising from the bale of hay.

"Is there a manual?" Richard asked, dragging the tarp to the ground.

"My English is not so good," Vogel said, walking out the door.

"But mine is," Richard said, following behind. "If you find it, I can study it at home."

Vogel gave a shrug and jerked his head in the direction of his home.

Richard followed him across the yard and through the farmhouse back door. He looked around the dark kitchen with its grime-coated windows and the ancient coiled flypaper hanging from the ceiling. A dingy curtain hung over a doorway that he guessed led to a pantry.

Vogel rummaged through the long drawer of a pine hutch cluttered with mismatched crockery. "I can't pay you for working on the tractor," he said. "But you can take home produce."

Richard hadn't even thought about payment. It was

the excitement of getting a vehicle on the road, or field as it happened to be, that attracted him. Unlike Tommy, who washed his father's car every Saturday, he would be working on a real motor.

A flat, yellowed book, titled *67 New Thrills in Tractor Operations*, landed on the kitchen table.

———————◆———————

"Jimmy Brown wants you to tell us when Vogel cries," Tommy said with a smirk as they walked Amy to Mr. Black's. Amy did the gardening for Mr. and Mrs. Black to earn extra spending money. She loved working with flowers.

Richard was on his way to the cemetery. He visited his father's grave once a week to pull up the weeds. If he didn't, no one would be able to find the flat lump of concrete, edges ragged with gravel and the worn letters, spelling out FULLER.

Mr. and Mrs. Black lived across the street from the cemetery. They were the first family on Maple Street to have a telephone installed. Since it was the only one close by they let the neighbours use it. The Blacks had no children, but they lit a jack-o-lantern on Halloween night and handed out small bags of fudge. A large Christmas tree filled their front window, every year.

"Why does he cry?" Amy asked.

Tommy's sister had a blaze of thick hair, like her brother's. She wore it pulled back in a single braid, but strands always escaped, surrounding her porcelain face with copper curls. Amy was a year older than Richard but they were in the same grade at school. She had been kept back, much to the horror of her parents, but Amy didn't seem to mind. She didn't seem to mind much about anything.

"Who knows," Tommy said. "Jimmy said Vogel sent him home without a penny."

"Jimmy probably bruised the fruit," Richard said.

"I don't get it," said Tommy

"That's because you don't know what it's like to bring in a harvest."

He would never forget the day the old Dutchman had handed him a first-picked peach. Mr. Vogel held one in his hand and felt the skin with his broad calloused thumb. Richard copied, feeling the tight fuzz. The old farmer said nothing, as he brought the Empire peach up to his nose. Richard did the same, drinking in the sweet smell of nectar, before they took a big juicy bite.

"Mr. Vogel is very particular about his produce."

The Blacks' house, similar to the Fullers', was a wooden two-storey box with a long, flat verandah. Unlike Richard's house, though, it regularly received a new coat of paint. Trellises of roses, morning glories, and sweet peas framed the verandah. A giant circular flowerbed filled the lawn and pots of geraniums marched up the stairs.

A small clapboard extension stood where the garage used to be. Mr. Black had rebuilt his kitchen to accommodate two new ovens, several bake tables, cupboards, and shelves.

"Poor Mr. Black," Amy said to Tommy and Richard on their way up the street. "He strained his back and he's not supposed to lift anything."

"How's he making his deliveries?" Richard asked.

"His nephew is helping," Amy said. She lowered her voice. "But he's kind of lazy."

As they walked up the driveway, Richard spotted the boy leaning back on a wooden chair against the side of the bake house. His flat cap covered his eyes.

"Hello. Richard," Mrs. Black called out from behind the screen door. Her soft, plump arms held a large wicker basket full of crispy bread in brown paper bags. "I haven't seen you around much this summer."

Richard ran to hold the screen door open. The aroma of baking wafted over him like a warm breeze. "I've been working," he said, walking her down the drive. "I got a job on a farm."

Mrs. Black's eyes widened with surprise. She blew away the dark curl that fell across her eye. Then she nodded in the direction of the black Ford with the long square snout.

Richard opened the back door of the car and gave a long, low whistle. The rear seat was gone. In its place was a slotted wooden rack. Mrs. Black placed the loaves in the slots.

"That should be enough to see him through his morning round," she commented. She smoothed down the front of her snowy white apron. Then she removed a bobby pin from her hair and pushed the loose curl back under her hair net. This pecan-skinned woman with the shiny black hair always made Richard think she had just stepped out of the oven, like a gingerbread lady.

"Did your husband put in that rack?" Richard asked.

Mrs. Black nodded. "There are shelves in the trunk," she told him, "and a special compartment to hold pies."

She walked around to the back of the car and lifted the trunk lid.

The built-in cupboard in the trunk had removable shelves. "This is where we put the special orders," she said. "You know, like wedding cakes."

Mrs. Black reached into the pocket of her apron and pulled out two pieces of paper. She removed the red thumbtack from the door of the cupboard and affixed a list. "These are the names of the customers and what they have ordered."

"This is the most amazing car I have ever seen," Richard said.

"You like it?" came a voice from behind. Mr. Black, a short stocky man with a large protruding stomach, clasped his hands over his stomach. He reminded Richard of a fat squirrel on haunches, staring out of gold circle glasses.

"Are we fully loaded?" he asked.

His wife nodded. "Here's your copy." She handed him his list and assisted him into the driver's seat, arranging a green brocade pillow behind him. "He's hurt his back," she explained to Richard and Tommy.

Everyone jumped at the blare of the car horn, everyone except the boy on the chair. He raised his cap from his eyes and then sauntered towards the car.

"The only thing that boy has to do is hop in and out of the car while I drive," Mr. Black complained to the three of them out the window. "And leave those cigarettes behind," he shouted. "No one wants a loaf of bread that stinks of cigarette smoke!"

Amy appeared behind the screen holding an empty pitcher. "Can I make Richard and Tommy some lemonade?" she asked through the screen.

Mrs. Black nodded and went back into the bakery.

"Let's pull up those weeds in the front garden," Richard suggested to Tommy. "That way Amy can get off work earlier."

Tommy scowled, but pitched in. By the time the lemonade was ready, two large bundles of limp greenery tied with string lay beside the porch steps.

Richard walked into his mother's kitchen that night with a loaf of freshly baked bread, and a half dozen jam tarts. The afternoon of weed pulling had burnished his skin and turned his hair flaxen. "I just might have myself another job," he told her.

Except for the sound of a wet wad of material slapping and sloshing up and down the washboard, the room was quiet. For a few minutes, his mother washed and rinsed in a steady determined way. Then she looked up. "You're not thinking of quitting school, are you?"

"Nah," Richard said, biting into one of the tarts.

Grace Fuller let out a heavy breath. "I know you dream about seeing the world," she said, drying her hands on her apron. "But you have to get yourself an education."

Richard stood at the side of the galvanized tub, munching. "Don't worry, Ma," he said through a mouthful of crumbs. "I'll work it out."

Grace turned her body to him, her work-worn face meeting his. "And what do you plan to do with all this money that you will be making?"

Richard spread out his hands in front of him. He spotted a few crumbs at the end of his fingers and sucked them off before replying. "Mr. Black can't pay me a lot, but I make tips." He didn't want to tell her about the bike.

He hoped it would bring a smile of surprise to her face when she saw it.

"What about Mr. Vogel?" his mother asked. "He's expecting you to pick late peaches."

"I know," Richard said.

With a smile, he thought about Mr. Black's words. "I'll use my nephew until you've picked your last peach. I'm very impressed by your loyalty and sense of commitment."

Richard went to his room at the back of the house on the second floor. He crawled under his bed and pulled out the thin square tin with the picture of a bearded sailor that he kept beneath a loose floorboard. He tossed in the dime Mrs. Black had given him for pulling the weeds. *This must be what it feels like to be a banker*, he thought, looking at the pile of bills and loose change.

Richard opened his dresser drawer and took the picture of his father out from underneath his socks. It used to sit on top of the china cabinet in the dining room, but when his mother sold the cabinet the movers broke the frame. Richard had rescued the photograph and kept it in his drawer ever since. Once in a while he found it on top of his socks.

He gazed at Arthur William Fuller in full army uniform. His father had sat for the photograph the day after he'd joined up. After he returned from war Richard was born. But Richard never got to know his dad. No one could believe he'd dodged all those bullets and shells to die of pneumonia in his own bed at home.

Richard smiled, knowing his father would be proud of the fact he was only $22.40 short of a brand new bike.

CHAPTER 4

Morse Code

Richard set his alarm for five thirty, but his eyes opened long before it rang. He put his hands behind his head, watched the sun rise through the lace curtains, and thought about all the places in Niagara Falls he was going to see that day.

His clothes, except for his shirt, lay across the walnut dining-room chair that served as his bedside table. When he got to the kitchen, a freshly ironed white one hung from the ironing board.

"Whose is that?" Richard asked.

"Found it in a load of towels from one of the hotels," his mother replied. "No way of knowing who it might belong to, so you might as well wear it."

Richard smiled. He'd never worn a crisp white shirt with a starched collar before. It made him feel important, kind of like being in charge. He was glad he'd taken the time to find his father's shoeshine kit in the basement and given his boots a good polish.

After putting a jam sandwich wrapped in wax paper and a small bottle of Borden's milk into his father's lunch box, he polished its aluminum sides until he could see his face.

Mr. and Mrs. Black sat on their front porch sipping morning tea from cups with saucers.

"You'll never make it through the first day of action," Mr. Black called out over the china rim. "That lunch pail reflects so much sun a sniper would take you down in a second."

Richard's smile faded as he stood at the bottom of the porch step.

"Stop that," Mrs. Black said to her husband, as she put down her tea cup. "This boy doesn't need any of your army survival tips." She walked down the steps and took the lunch pail from Richard's hand. "You look very nice Richard," she said, "and you don't need to bring a lunch." She glanced over her shoulder and scowled at her smiling husband. "The morning route ends back here. We all have lunch together and then fill the car for the afternoon route."

The deliveries started with a neighbourhood full of massive oaks, manicured lawns, and stone houses. Many of them had magnificent walkways, gardens, and cars in the driveways.

"Here," Mr. Black instructed. "We deliver to the back door."

In the next neighbourhood they delivered to the front door. Richard noticed lamps with lace doilies over their shades, pianos, and fresh flowers on hall tables.

All morning Richard took the items from the car as Mr. Black directed. He darted up the steps, past empty milk bottles, sunning cats, and barking dogs to deliver bread, pies, cakes, and tarts. By Richard's standards, all of Mr. Black's customers were well off. Most of them didn't bother taking their change. Richard held it out, but they just smiled and waved it away.

At noon, Richard experienced a lunch unlike anything he had known before. Mrs. Black's carrots sparkled as if they were made of sugar. Mashed potatoes billowed out of the bowl, and the roast beef swam in creamy gravy.

"You forgot to tell me what the doctor said about your back yesterday," Mrs. Black said.

"One word," her husband mumbled as he helped himself to more mashed potatoes. "One word was all he said."

"And what might that one word be?" Mrs. Black asked.

Richard ran several words through his mind as he waited to hear the doctor's.

"Diet," Mr. Black said before tucking into his second helping. The buttons on his striped shirt strained. He looked at Richard and smiled. "Looks like you've never had that problem."

"Nope," Richard replied. "My mother wonders how I manage to stay so skinny with all the eating I do." He didn't repeat the part about her being glad other people were helping to fill his hollow leg.

"He also told me I had one of two choices, either stop baking the most delicious bread in town, or stop eating it," Mr. Black continued.

"But that's way more than one word," Amy protested.

Mrs. Black, serving ice-cream, laughed. "More than one word and more than one helping," she said, placing a dish of twin creamy mounds in front of Richard.

For Richard, it was his first taste of real ice cream. His mother had always called the frozen top of the milk ice cream. He ate it, but never understood what all the fuss was about. Mrs. Black's creamy frozen dessert, however, didn't taste anything at all like that.

After reloading the car and collecting the special orders phoned in that morning, Richard and Mr. Black set out to make their deliveries to the south end of the city.

"I won't need you the last two weeks of July," Mr. Black announced when they began the afternoon route. "Looks like you'll have some farm time before school anyway."

"Are you and Mrs. Black going on holiday?" Richard asked.

"I'm off to camp," Mr. Black informed him. "My brother and his lazy son cover for me."

"You're going camping?" Richard asked. He couldn't conjure a picture of Mr. Black sitting on a log roasting wieners over a fire.

"Army camp," Mr. Black replied. "The Lincoln and Welland Regiment train in Niagara-on-the-Lake each year."

"What kind of training?" Richard asked.

"Communications," Mr. Black replied. "Sending messages on the field, by flag, radio, and telegraph." He slowed the car to a stop at the sign and turned to Richard. His eyes lit with excitement. "The trainees use the rifle ranges, practice marching, and set up signal stations at different places. You know Morse code, don't you?"

Richard shook his head.

As Mr. Black drove, he said. "All important news comes by telegraph, you know."

Richard nodded. Whenever his mother saw the telegraph boy on the street, she'd say, "It's birth, death, or marriage."

"Knowing how to run a telegraph could get you a good-paying job on a train or ship."

Richard thought about the steamer at Queenston.

"I learned the code as an artillery man during the First World War. I served in Europe first, then in northern Russia for the Bolshevik uprising."

"How long were you in Russia?" Richard asked in awe.

"From September 1918 until June 1919," he replied. "Then I returned to Canada."

"My dad was an army man," Richard told him.

"I know. And a fine soldier he was," Mr. Black said with a nod of his head. He pulled the car to the side of the roadway while Richard adjusted the baker's back pillow.

"How do I learn Morse code?"

"Well, now," the baker said with a smile. He lifted his hands from the wheel and rubbed them together. "I can teach you that."

"What are you training for this time?" Richard asked.

The large man in the driver's seat threw back his head and roared with laughter.

"I'm afraid my training days are over, my boy," he said. "I'm the cook! Why don't you come and see the camp for yourself? It would give your mother a day out."

CHAPTER 5

The Demonstration

Mr. Black extended the invitation to Richard's mother for the two of them to accompany him and his wife to the opening ceremonies at Niagara-on-the-Lake. Richard's brown pants held a knife-like crease, and his plaid cotton shirt was spotless. His mother wore her grey suit, black hat, and white gloves.

Mrs. Black appeared in a flowered chiffon dress. The blue feather on her hat matched her elbow-length gloves. Mr. Black dressed in his best blue suit, as he was no longer able to button up the jacket of his army uniform.

When they arrived at the Niagara-on-the-Lake military camp that hot summer afternoon, the cavalry rode the common, bands practiced, and troops flowed like the Niagara River.

"The Lincoln and Welland Regiment, the Argyll and Sutherland Highlanders, and the Dufferin and Haldimand Rifles are all here for the summer," Mr. Black told them.

"I didn't know there would be horses," Richard exclaimed. He stopped to watch them gallop in formation, stop, wheel about, and begin again.

"Those Royal Canadian Dragoons are P.F."

Richard had to smile. Mr. Black always used initials when talking about the army. "What's P.F.?" he asked.

"Permanent Force," Mr. Black replied. He pointed to the regal officer on a huge white horse crossing the green. "Camp commandant, Colonel Elwood Ford, and M.C.D.S.O.," he informed Richard. "Everyone stays out of his way."

Richard nodded. He didn't bother to ask what all those initials meant. With that many, he knew the man was important.

The crowd, sitting in stands around the grassy common, watched horses jump rail fences and bales of hay. Then soldiers removed the fences and the area filled with army trucks and small track vehicles. As the roar of the single-engined biplanes echoed across the sky, everyone looked up. Mr. Black pointed to the pin-pricks of red, green, and white in arrow formation as they swooped through the clouds. "They've come from the air force base in Trenton," he told Richard. "I knew this would be something to see."

A voice from the loudspeaker crackled. "These fellows do pin-point photography for artillery observation."

All eyes scanned the sky.

"Their job is to locate arsenals, troop assemblies, or batteries of guns."

One of the aircraft flew low. A small bundle fell to the ground and exploded into a puff of white. The crowd reacted with awe and applause.

"Part of the navigator's training," the voice explained, "is to calculate the proper point to operate the bomb release. No actual bombs will be used today," he assured the crowd, "but the camera on the ground will record the plane's drop.

These boys will find out later if they hit their target."

Several men ran out on to the field carrying poles, canvas, axles, and a set of tires.

"Watch our men construct a target vehicle before your very eyes," the announcer said.

Within minutes a large canvas truck appeared in the middle of the field.

"How about that?" asked the announcer, encouraging the audience's applause. "Now all we need is some gas."

To the amusement of those in the stands, a man dressed in khaki overalls wandered out on to the field carrying a can of gas. Shading his eyes to the sun, he looked from side to side in search of the truck.

"Looks like this lad hasn't done his navigation homework," the announcer said. "He'll need some help finding his way."

The crowd complied, calling directions out to the man on the field. Catching sight of the false truck with exaggerated surprise, he placed the can of gas inside the canvas and scurried away.

"With a wing span of forty feet, and a cruising speed of 206 miles per hour, the sting of this fighter plane is its guns," the announcer said to the mesmerized crowd. "The Hawker Hurricane's pilot has the combined firing power of eight, that's right, I said eight machine guns."

The full-throated roar of a powerful engine filled the sky. The fighter plane flew towards the stands, making the crowds duck before it pulled back up into the heavens.

Then the fighter plane returned and zoomed towards the truck. A barrage of bullets chewed up the grass around it, tearing huge holes in the canvas.

The crowd screamed and cheered when the target truck exploded into flames.

As the plane flew over the horizon, one of the commanding officers moved along the base of the wooden stands, inviting able-bodied young men to ride the demonstration vehicles. He spied Richard in the crowd and called up to him. "You! There! Why aren't you in the army?"

Richard's mother placed one of her gloved hands on Richard's chest and grabbed his arm with the other in an attempt to make the officer back off. But he didn't.

"Such a fine specimen of a young man," the officer bellowed. "How about taking a ride in one of the very latest army vehicles?" He looked around at the crowd and gave a large wink.

Richard wanted to ride, but the pressure of his mother clutching his arm made him shake his head in refusal.

"The Canadian Army has extended you an invitation, sir!" the man in the red-banded hat bellowed out to all around. Many in the crowd laughed. "The Canadian Army is not used to having its invitations turned down, sir!"

Two soldiers wearing yellow armbands with the white letters "MP" hustled Richard out of his mother's arms, down the steps, and into a small vehicle. Richard grinned and gave a shrug.

The military police set off at top speed. The vehicle, reeking of oil, bounced across the hoof-pocked grounds. The powerful noise of airplane motors once again echoed across the sky, bringing everyone to a hush.

Just as the vehicle came around a hill of hay, a flour bomb landed on the hood, exploding into a cloud of white. The MPs leaped out except for Richard. He fell out and rolled along the ground. There he lay still, covered in flour.

The crowd screamed and moaned.

Grace Fuller rose with her hands to her mouth.

Mrs. Black put both her arms around her.

A Red Cross ambulance rushed on to the field with its siren wailing. Two men hopped out, picked Richard up, and flung him on to the stretcher.

"They shouldn't be so rough with him," Mrs. Black protested, "especially if …" She stopped speaking, unsure as to what word to use next.

The ambulance travelled the entire circuit of the field, instead of heading off to the hospital as everyone expected. It came to a full stop in front of the stands.

Before Grace Fuller could gather her senses and make her way down, the back door of the ambulance opened. Richard jumped out as clean as a whistle waving the Union Jack.

The crowd cheered and whooped as the demonstration ended.

———◆———

"Mr. Black is relying on my youthful spirit of adventure to accept the challenge of training," Richard explained to his mother that night in their kitchen. "Those were his exact words."

His mother kept her hands in the dishwater but had stopped cleaning the plates. Then she lifted them, wiped them on her apron, and turned her thin face towards him.

"Isn't picking fruit and delivering bread every spare minute enough?" she asked.

But Richard couldn't hear his mother. The voice in his head belonged to Mr. Black. "You'd have no trouble getting a job on a ship, once you learn wireless telegraphy."

Training like that, Richard knew, could only bring money, travel, and adventure.

CHAPTER 6

Camp Niagara

The next morning, Richard got off the army bus with Mr. Black and followed him to the long line of men waiting outside the flaps of a white tent. Hundreds of these tents had sprung up like daisies overnight on the grassy common. Military personnel crossed back and forth between them.

"You're one lucky young man," Mr. Black told him, clapping Richard on the back. "It's not often someone doesn't show up, leaving a last minute space."

Richard grinned. It took a lot of talking before his mother finally agreed to let him go to the camp for two weeks. After his part in the demonstration, he felt like Superman. He might even try riding one of those cavalry horses.

Mr. Black waited with him in line. When it was Richard's turn to register, he reached down and tapped a name on the list. The officer nodded and put a check mark next to it without looking up. Mr. Black leaned in and whispered into Richard's ear. "All you have to remember," he said, "is your name."

Richard smiled at the joke until Mr. Black cleared his throat and announced, "Private Chester Lee Houston, reporting for duty, sir." Then he nodded at Richard and turned and walked away.

Richard looked about in confusion. That wasn't his name. But before he could straighten the officer out, another soldier ordered him to step aside into the next line.

He followed the line of men towards a row of tents hoping he would remember to answer to this new name. The soldier pointed out the gun park, vehicle lines, and classrooms along the way. Passing a tent crowded with men, Richard strained to see inside as a soldier dispensed soft drinks, chocolate bars, chewing gum, and cigarettes. "Canteen," the soldier called out as they passed, but it was of no importance to Richard. He didn't plan on spending any money. At the end of this week he hoped to put several bills into the thin square tin under the floorboard. One dollar and thirty cents a day was far more than he would make staying home and picking fruit.

At the next tent he received a blanket, wash basin, and a small stack of clothes. "These are your fatigues," the corporal told him, slapping a white pith helmet on top of the pile. "Remember, no hard hats after dark."

They marched down the row of tents. "Drop your gear here," the corporal told him, stopping in front of a tent marked with the number five. "These are your quarters."

Richard pushed back the tent flap to see six cots, three on either side. Two men were already inside. One was lying on his cot reading a newspaper. The other polished his boots.

"Excuse me, sirs," Richard said, his voice cracking as he spoke.

The man behind the newspaper ignored him. The one

polishing his boots looked up. His hair was jet black, a little too black, Richard noticed. It was almost the same colour as the polish on his boots. He fixed his large gooseberry eyes on Richard.

"Jeez," he said. "They're getting younger every day." He put his boot down and wiped his hands on the rag. "What are you, twelve?"

Before Richard could reply, a voice came from behind the newspaper. "Sirs?" the voice repeated as the man lowered the newspaper. His plumpish face had a piano-keyboard smile. "Either you are one polite kid or you've got yourself in the wrong tent. We're all privates here, no sirs." He looked Richard up and down. "He does look young," he admitted to the guy polishing his boots.

Richard claimed the cot farthest from the front and went back outside. Beneath a canopy roof, in a classroom of folding tables and chairs, Richard took his first elementary test along with the rest of the new trainees.

"Experienced in signalling, I see," the officer commented after Richard responded in perfect Morse code. Richard smiled. It wasn't any different from the games he and Mr. Black played with their fingers on the dash board while making deliveries.

A junior officer marched the men around him to another classroom in the training tent line, but Richard was told to remain behind.

Soon others filled the empty chairs. Richard glanced about. Everyone was much older; some old enough to be his father.

A tall, bony, uniformed man entered the classroom tent and strode to the front. "A signalman is a fully trained expert," he began, "competent in every branch of signalling and in the installation of all necessary equipment."

Richard cupped his head in his hands focusing on the tight-skinned man's face. Dark brown hair plastered his scalp. His moustache was so well formed it almost looked false.

"I am Sergeant Gifford from the signal training centre in Barriefield," he said, as he pulled out an empty chair and put his polished boot on the seat. "Every now and again they let one of us senior officers out to honeymoon in Niagara."

There were a few twitters of laughter among the crowd.

Sergeant Gifford pulled a stack of small black notebooks from the table beside him and indicated to a fellow in front they were to pass them about. "But," he paused dramatically, making sure all eyes were on him, "a signalman must first and foremost be a soldier. You will learn to march, obey orders, and handle a rifle. You will keep your equipment clean."

"Yes sir!" Richard called out before he could stop himself. He closed his eyes in embarrassment expecting the instructor to come down on him with a swoop. But he didn't.

"Soldiers?" the officer called out to the rest.

"Yes sir," the men in the tent chorused.

Lunch was nothing like he had come to expect working for Mr. Black. Richard dropped on to the grass with a tin tray holding a square of cheese, a slice of bread, a dollop of red jam, and a tin mug of tea.

"More bread if you want it," the man handing out the trays told him.

"Great," replied Richard, closing his eyes thinking he would soon be sinking his teeth into a snowy white slice of one of Mr. Blacks crusty loaves. But this bread was dark and doughy; he had to use his tea to wash it down.

Training continued until supper. Richard marched from classroom to classroom. Dinner was sausages and mashed potatoes, with vanilla pudding on another tin tray.

At night, Richard lay on his narrow rock-like cot, reading the discarded newspaper while the others sat outside the tent, playing cards, smoking, and passing flasks. They were to be up for a morning run at five. He didn't even get up that early for school.

At first they all thought it was a joke when they arrived at the common the next morning. Seven pedal bikes right out of the 1920s, with straight frames, large tires, and brakes on the handlebars, stood in a row. But as soon as they heard that pedalling these monsters around the fringe of the common was their first lesson in learning to ride a motorbike, everyone hopped on.

The instructors stood in the middle of the circle waving people off as they decided who was good enough to go the next step. That afternoon, after taking a few turns around the square on the motorbike, two of the instructors took Richard for a spin along the highway.

"You should have seen me," Richard told Mr. Black when he found him behind the officers' cook tent. "One soldier ahead of me and a soldier behind me," he shouted. "I even rode along Highway 2!"

"Wait until your mother hears you rode a motorcycle," Mr. Black said with a hearty laugh.

Richard didn't reply. He hadn't planned on telling her.

CHAPTER 7

Signalling

"Signalling is essential to the performance of a large body of troops," the instructor began the next morning, "whether you are in training or on the battlefield."

"Think there'll be war?" a voice called out from the back. "Someone needs to whip that Hitler fellow into shape."

The instructor ignored the comment. "You are here today to learn the mysteries of line." He held up a small metal suitcase. "This is what we use for wireless telegraphy." He patted the radio on the table next to him. "If you are good," the officer told the class, "you will get to work with Wireless Set No. 19." He held it up with a contented sigh. "The model of the future."

Richard sat back in his chair and smiled. He could just see Tommy's face if he got his hands on one of those for the tree house.

"In the meantime," the instructor informed them, "learning by doing is the guiding principle of training. Gunners, today we lay wire."

A truck dropped Richard and two other men off near a clump of trees on the steep rise of the 1812 battlefield, west of the village of Niagara-on-the-Lake.

Vincent Butler, an enormous, hairy man with large fingers like bananas, went by the nickname Ape. Albert Kennedy, a gentleman in every sense, worked with piano-playing fingers. The driver handed Ape a large spool of wire. "You've got to lay and conceal a half-mile of signal wire to battalion headquarters," he told them. He handed Al the battery-operated telephone. "Then transmit this message," he said, handing Richard a sealed envelope.

The blue sky rose before them as they walked the rise of the hill unwinding the wire. Just before they reached the top, a Royal Canadian Dragoon rode up beside them on horseback. Richard couldn't take his eyes off the beautiful brown gelding with black mane and tail as it galloped past. The horseman stopped at the top of the hill and climbed up onto his saddle. He used flags to send a message to the other Dragoons at the bottom of the road.

"Wow," Richard said in awe of the flags flashing above rows of shining gold buttons.

The Dragoon ignored them and dropped back into the saddle. Then he rode off to a small wooden shed by the road. He stood on his saddle, paused for a moment, and climbed up on to the roof. From there he gave another magnificent display of flag waving to those on the common.

But to everyone's surprise, the shed, with a loud groan of timber, collapsed into a cloud of dust.

The horse, frightened by the commotion, ran off. Richard, Al, and Ape could only stare with mouths open. When they finally rushed to his side, the Dragoon rose from the pile of broken boards.

"Don't you dare to laugh," he commanded, as he dusted himself off.

No one did, but the merry look in Richard's blue eyes angered the Dragoon. He strode into the middle of the road and whistled for his horse. Seeing what they were doing, the Dragoon leaned down to the spool of wire on the road and gave it a hard yank. It jumped and bounced all the way back down the hill and fell into the ravine, where it was impossible to retrieve.

Horrified, Richard, Al, and Ape watched the Dragoon mount his horse and ride away.

"No wire," Ape said, slumping against the fence by the side of the road. "We're beat."

Richard and Al stood with their hands on their hips wondering what to do.

"Wait a minute," Richard said. "The fence is made of wire."

"You can't expect us to tear down a fence," Albert said, twisting his hands about.

"We don't have to tear it down," Richard said. "If I am not mistaken, this fence runs right past headquarters. We just have to hook a wire up to it."

He told Ape to head back to headquarters, find some wire, and lay a short line to the fence.

Richard connected the radio wire to the fence. He and Al curled up in the ditch by the side of the road and waited. Within half an hour, they had made contact with Ape and sent their message.

If the signal officer hadn't come across the empty spool of wire on his way to inspect, they wouldn't have had to explain. But, instead of getting into trouble, they received hearty congratulations for their ingenuity.

As the week progressed, Richard studied *The Manual*

of Military Law, learned *The King's Regulations*, practiced, drilled, ate, and slept.

On the second last day of camp, his unit marched to the rifle ranges.

"A signaller on the field lives with his rifle," their instructor told them. "He must be ready to defend himself and know how to shoot."

Richard almost dropped the thick, smelly weapon put into his arms. He never expected it to have such a weight and such a powerful odour of oil. He looked down the long, straight barrel and lifted it to his chest as he'd been instructed. When he fired, he staggered backwards. Richard recovered from the unexpected recoil, rubbed his shoulder, and managed to fire off a few rounds.

The hot sun, dusty road, and the ache in his shoulder, made Richard think he would never make it back to their tent. But as they came within sight of the camp gate, the waiting regimental band played them in. The music seemed to give Richard the extra energy needed to lift his head and march on as the commandant took the salute.

That night they received the assignment to set up a signal station on one side of the grassy common and communicate with camp headquarters the next morning.

"Here is your message," the signal sergeant said, handing Richard an envelope. He was a full head taller than Richard and as big around as a barrel.

At the crack of dawn, Richard, Ape, and Alfred took up a spot on the lower ground about three miles away from headquarters. Al opened a wooden case and removed the battery-operated lamp that reminded Richard of a large bicycle light. He raised the metal hood that protected the spotlight and fiddled with the small knob in the centre of the lens to adjust the brightness. Ape positioned the telescope for the return signal. Richard translated their message into the correct series of dots and dashes and called it out.

Their signal lamp winked across the landscape. When their response came back, Richard translated, just as the thunderclouds rolled in. They made their way back to the mess tent in the pouring rain, proud of their success.

At the close of the camp, the major-general gave a speech. "I had two goals for this camp," he said. "The first was to have as many well-trained men as possible. I am pleased to announce all signallers qualified first class." He brought his arm up to the vicinity of his face and waved it to his right in a congratulatory salute to the gunners before him.

"My second goal was to pick up some of the prize money offered by the government. That we will find out once all camp results are in." He leaned forward and smiled. "I hope to see all of you again next year. Good show, men!"

Richard slept in the back of the army bus all the way home, his hand inside his pocket, clutching his pay packet.

CHAPTER 8

Gunner Fuller

Richard returned to Vogel's farm when he finished camp. As he had hoped, he found the crates in the tractor shed jammed with parts. He spent most of his free time over the month of September on his back underneath the tractor, hoping to have it running before it got too cold to work in the shed.

———◆———

Mr. McLaughlin, Tommy's father, herded Richard and his mother into the back seat of his car early Sunday morning for church. Usually everyone sat together, but lately adults filled the pews. The youngest children had to sit on the floor in front. The older ones stood in the back.

"My friends," the minister began at the end of the service. He stood at the front in a pool of coloured light coming from the stained glass windows above. A picture of King George sat on a table in front of the altar, flanked by the Union Jack and the Canadian Red Ensign. "For those who do not know," he said, "Hitler demands Danzig be returned to Germany or he'll invade Poland."

A profound silence fell over those in the church.

The minister cleared his throat and wiped his forehead with a handkerchief. "It is tempting to give way to anger," he said. "But I urge you to think of how Jesus forgave those who placed him on the cross. We must prepare our souls for this great conflict. Let us pray."

"What's a damn zig?" Amy asked, tugging at Richard's arm as they got out of the church. "Why does Germany want it back? And how did they lose it, anyway?"

"It's a city which used to be part of Germany," Richard explained. "The League of Nations made it a free port the first time the Germans made trouble." He knew this because Mr. Black tossed war information around daily. "The Germans want access to water." Richard turned to Tommy. "Great Britain won't tolerate Germany invading Poland," he said, repeating Mr. Black's exact words in a serious voice.

"Holy mackerel," Tommy shouted. "That Hitler guy must be trying to take over the world. Let's go listen to our radio."

"You go ahead without me," Richard said. He was never comfortable when they tried to huddle in the McLaughlins' silent, lemon-polished room used only for special occasions. When their cathedral radio crackled like bacon in a frying pan, Amy had to turn it off. The noise gave her mother a headache.

Richard knew his mother wouldn't bother with their small black hump of a radio when she got home. "No point in feeding off bad news," she always said, turning it off when Richard was trying to listen.

"I'm heading over to see Mr. Black," he said. "I'll catch up with you later."

The rotund baker heaved himself out of his chair when Richard appeared in the doorway.

"Did you hear the news?" Richard asked.

"It looks grim," Mr. Black said. "It will mean war with Britain for sure."

"The Commonwealth," Richard said, straightening his shoulders, "will need soldiers."

"You're not thinking …" Mr. Black said, catching the look on Richard's face.

"I have to enlist," Richard said in a strangled voice. "You did. Mr. Vogel did. My own father did."

"But we were all much older at the time," the baker argued.

A determination came over Richard as if Mr. Black had flipped a switch. "Mr. Vogel came from a farm, you were working in a bakery, and my father left trade school. None of you had the training I had," he said.

"You better talk it over with your mother first," Mr. Black said, putting his hand on Richard's shoulder. But Richard had no intention of doing that.

◆

The officer from Camp Niagara shuffled the pile of papers on top of the scarred wooden table. When Richard strolled in, he looked up and grinned. "So Houston, we meet again." He made a wide sweep with his arm until his fingers touched his temple in salute, and then dropped them down. "Are you signing up?"

"Yes sir," Richard said, pushing his library card across the desk. He had to get rid of the name that got him into training camp.

The sergeant read the card and blinked. "You changed your name?"

"My mother remarried," Richard said with a stutter. "That was my step-father's name."

"You didn't keep your father's name?" the sergeant asked in surprise. "Most boys do."

"This is my father's name," Richard said, stabbing the card in front of the sergeant. "I took a different one because my mother remarried, but changed it back."

"Good for you," the sergeant said, writing the word Fuller on the form. He paused and looked at the card again. "You changed your first name too?"

"That was always my first name," Richard blurted out. His face grew hot. "I mean," he stammered, "I was going by my middle name before."

Several men carrying cardboard suitcases crowded through the doorway and formed a noisy line behind Richard. The recruitment officer had no more time for talk. He ticked off a few boxes and added his signature to the bottom of several blank papers. "Fill them in and sign," he said, handing Richard the sheaf.

The soldier at the next desk took the completed forms from him. "Good luck," he said. "You'll receive your joining orders in the next couple of days."

◆

"What's that in your hand?" his mother asked when the letter arrived at the door.

"Look, Ma," Richard said, holding it in the air away from her. "In the army, I'll get paid a lot more. It's a lot better than picking fruit or delivering bread."

Grace snatched the letter and read it. Her hand went to her heart as she took a step backward. "Why on earth would you want to join up?" she asked in a quiet voice.

"The higher your rank, the more you get paid," Richard went on. "As a private I would make a dollar thirty a day. Since I went to camp, they've made me a gunner and I'll make a dollar fifty."

"You know it's a twenty-four hour day," she argued. "Not an eight hour one."

"I get all my clothing and meals," he said, snatching the letter back.

"And no overtime," she continued. "What do you know about being a soldier?"

"I know a lot," Richard replied with a jerk of his head. "I've got training."

"All you know is crawling around in the dirt playing with radios." Grace returned to her ironing board, collapsed it, and put it against the wall.

"It's a privilege to be able to serve my country," Richard said in a loud, arrogant voice.

His mother leaned against the porcelain lip of the sink and folded her arms. "Is it a privilege to sleep in a tent, use an outhouse, and eat meals off a tin tray?" she asked. "And is it a privilege to get shot?"

From that day on, Grace Fuller stopped speaking to her son.

Richard stopped trying to think up ways to change his mother's mind. *That would be like attacking Germans with one of her hat pins.* He became nothing more than a ghost haunting his own home.

———————◆———————

The gearshift clanked like a hammer pounding iron. The engine managed a steady twenty miles an hour on a flat grade but a small hill made the ride an adventure. It took Richard over two hours to plough a single acre. His heart rose at the sight of the furrows between the fruit trees and the smell of freshly turned soil. Richard realized, as he sat in the middle of the field, that the orchard was beautiful in any season.

The last thing Richard said to Mr. Vogel was, "The dials on the dashboard will look frozen until she takes time to warm up. You know how to jiggle the gears."

The farmer gave him a long stare as he stroked his beard. Then he placed his hand on Richard's shoulder and said, "It looks like we're in for a nasty storm. You better take care of yourself."

———————◆———————

Richard stowed his pocket knife with the antler handle in his rucksack, along with all the underwear and socks that he owned.

With a tiny click, he unlatched and lowered the top of the desk in the living room. Two stamps in an empty cough drop tin sat on an unused blotting pad next to a dry bottle of ink. He opened the small drawer at the top, removed an envelope, and put all the money he had saved for his bike inside. He propped it up in front of the sewing machine.

After he shut the front door, Richard leaned against it and took a deep breath. *This will be no different from going to training camp*, he told himself as he walked towards the train station in the early dawn. School seemed so far away and so unimportant; after all, he was now a soldier serving his country.

CHAPTER 9

Spaghetti Villa

R ichard stepped off the train into a bitter November wind sweeping off Lake Ontario. Kingston, built almost entirely of grey limestone, seemed to be wall to wall servicemen. Every kind of military personnel hung about the shops, walked the streets, and filled the wooden city benches.

He clutched the neck of his greatcoat as he followed the river of men uphill to Vimy Barracks. A relic from the Crimean war, its pleated back, designed to cover the end of a horse, reached the ground. Not wishing to hurt Mr. Black's feelings, Richard had accepted it, and was now very glad that he had.

Entering the building, the smells of damp wool, cigarette smoke, and stale beer engulfed him. "Gunner Fuller," the sergeant-major said when Richard reported in. "They are expecting you in Barriefield."

"Barriefield," Richard repeated in surprise. "Why?"

"Signal training centre," the officer replied. "Catch the next truck out."

North of the Montreal highway, Camp Barriefield was nothing but a collection of wooden huts with canvas siding. A single light bulb dangled from a cord above the iron beds with a bench at each end.

"You are financially responsible for everything issued," the quartermaster told all the newly inducted men. He slapped a list on top of their first stack of clothes. "Items marked with two asterisks will be issued to you in your company."

Richard looked at the only item on the list marked with asterisks, identification tags.

Battledress included shirts, trousers, two rolls of puttees, two pairs of socks, and a pair of big-toed boots. The coarse, brown, woolen tunic had a row of brass buttons down the front. With the cuff of his shirt, he rubbed the brass badge that sat above the peak of the cap.

The morning began with the sharp clear call of a bugle followed by roll call on the parade square. A junior commanding officer marched them to classrooms in the training wing. They received instruction in visual telegraphy, battery operated telephones, map reading, and orienteering. The route marches, assault course, and drills made Richard fitter and leaner and hungrier.

"You look familiar," Sergeant Gifford commented to Richard. "Are you from the west?"

Richard shook his head. "No, sir," he said. "We met at Camp Niagara."

"I was wondering if that's why you haven't put in for your leave," the sergeant said. "The train journey uses up all of the westerners' time. That's why they remain in barracks."

Richard just shrugged. He hadn't bothered with leave, knowing it wouldn't be for very long and a visit home wouldn't be comfortable.

It wasn't long before word passed they were to attend a "special parade."

"Gentlemen," the major told them all. "I have received a request for signallers overseas."

Richard's heart jumped.

"But, unless you sign one of these pink slips and go willingly, you aren't shipping out."

Richard signed on the spot.

The doctor jammed a cold stethoscope against Richard's chest. "Cough," he said. "Now stick out your tongue."

Richard moved to the next man who pulled out a tape measure. "Chest," he called out to the woman in uniform. "Thirty-two inches."

"Tattoos?" she asked.

The medical man looked at Richard and raised his eyebrows in question.

He shook his head.

Richard watched the barber trim moustaches to perfect little points, clip away curly mops, and turn the tops of heads into thatched roofs before he too lost his blonde shock.

After reading an eye chart, the man shoved a paper into his hands. "Sign at the x," he directed. Then he took Richard by the elbow to a small table. "Wait here for your needles."

Richard received two needles, one in the arm, and another in the chest. One needle was bad enough, but the two at once made him woozy. As he lay on a cot in the medical room, talk flew about him. Rumours were the frontline units badly needed reinforcements.

"We're going to Egypt to help the Arabs guard the Sewage Canal," one man said.

"It's not the Sewage Canal, you idiot," another called out. "It's the Suez Canal."

Richard received a railway voucher and a directive to report to the armouries in St. Catharines.

◆

"Welcome to Spaghetti Villa." The heavily accented French-Canadian voice greeted Richard at the doorway of the abandoned macaroni factory at the corner of Tasker and Welland. Tobacco smoke filled a room that smelled of sour beer. Men stood in groups throwing darts and sat around scarred wooden tables playing cards amid glasses of amber liquid.

He held his breath, doing his best not to cough as he made his way through the mass of male bodies. Shouts rang out above the buzz of male conversation as Richard checked the order board.

◆

In the crisp morning December air, they paraded in marching order in front of their barracks and then through the back streets of St. Catharines to the train station. There, they broke rank to say goodbye to family and friends. In the sea of khaki some wives tried to hold their husbands back while children chased each other about. Richard stood waiting to board. He reached up out of habit to push away the blond shock of hair that usually fell across his forehead.

"There he is," a small voice called out. "Hey! Richard!"

Tommy, along with Amy, ran up to him. Mr. and Mrs. Black followed.

"How did you know where to find me?" Richard asked with a huge grin.

"Army connections," Mr. Black replied with a smile just as big.

"I saw policemen on horses," Tommy said, "and ..."

Amy put her gloved hand over her brother's mouth. Then she twirled in her open-toed shoes with small heels for Richard to admire her lace-trimmed dress with tiny heart-shaped pockets. Her shiny copper hair played loose about her shoulders.

Richard gave a long, low whistle.

Mrs. Black's eyes shone seeing Richard for the first time in his black boots, knee-high puttees, khaki breeches, brass-buttoned tunic, and cap. She put her arm around him and drew him in for a hug. "It's as if my own son is leaving," she said in a tight voice.

Mr. Black put his hands on Richard's shoulders and looked him in the face. Richard could see the admiration in his eyes. "Step carefully," he said, "and always swing a long stick."

Giggling at Mr. Black's words, Amy handed Richard a shoebox tied with brown string.

"What's this?" he asked as his thumbs rested on the backs of her soft, warm hands.

"Envelopes, paper, and pens," Amy said. "No excuse not to write."

"Thanks," was all Richard could think to say as the crowd pushed them all closer. He felt her soft breath and smelled her lily of the valley perfume. Warmth spread up his arms, making his heart race.

"I have to go," he said at the whistle of the train.

Amy smiled and waved as Richard boarded the train. The image of his mother's pursed lips and disapproving look was forgotten.

CHAPTER 10

The *Empress of Britain*

As the troop train sped eastward towards the sea, Richard slept. At Rivière du Loup they stopped for a route march to get exercise. In Moncton, three other batteries boarded, completing the mobilization of the 1st Canadian Infantry Division.

The shouting call, "All troops derail," echoed along the lines inside the Halifax railroad shed followed by the din of men's voices. Richard grabbed his kit bag and stepped onto the platform. The orders "fall in" caused the tunnelled area to fill with the sound of shuffling feet. The yelled command, "Quick march," brought all footsteps in unison.

Stepping through the foggy morning air, Richard stopped to crane his neck to see how far the *Empress of Britain*, the ship he was about to board, rose into the clouds.

"Hey kid," a voice yelled out from behind. "You gonna spend all day gawking, or get yourself going?"

The gangways leading from the dock to the ships crawled with troops. When Richard reached the top, he felt the rise and fall of the sea beneath his feet. A ship's officer handed him a destination card. Holding it in his teeth, he joined the others at the rail.

With no bands, no flags, and no cheering crowds gathered to watch, the first of Canada's fighting forces set their course into the grey mist. The powerful escort of cruisers, destroyers, and submarines moved out of the harbour one by one. The most heavily armed units of the navy had the job of guarding the five slate-grey ships in the North Atlantic.

Richard wound his way through the ship, stopping to stare in the doorways of the stateroom, ballroom, bar rooms, and lounges. Within the polished wood-panelled walls of the dining room were round tables set for eight that sparkled with crystal stemware and silver cutlery. He thought of how impressed his mother would be with the starched white tablecloths and folded linen napkins. Richard decided this must be where the officers ate.

After clambering down several sets of stairs to the lower deck, Richard checked his card one more time and found his cabin. As he tossed his gear beside one of the twin beds, the sound of a flushing toilet made him turn.

"Hello there," a tall young man with brown hair called out when he emerged. He wore a long-sleeved collarless jersey over a pair of khaki trousers. "There's no porthole. It looks like we're on one of the inner decks." He finished wiping the shaving cream from his face and turned to toss the snow-white towel into the sink. A Pocket Book Company novel stuck out of his back pocket. He looked more like a student than a soldier.

"My name is Jack," he said, sticking out his hand. "Jack Gill, from St. Catharines."

A broad grin spread across Richard's face. Shaking Jack's hand with vigour, he replied, "Close to my home town, Niagara Falls. My name's Richard Fuller."

"Hah," Jack said, putting his hands on his hips. "Looks like they've put us fruit pickers together." He surveyed Richard from top to toe. "How come I haven't seen you before?"

"I've been in Barriefield," Richard told him, removing his cap.

"Ahh," Jack said. "I'm bunking with a 'sig.'" He tossed the towel on to his bed. "I won't hold that against you. Come on and meet the rest of the battery."

Jack poked his head into each of the rooms to introduce his bunkmate.

"Get inside and close the door," a man in the last room ordered. "We're starting a game."

Here, the bedside lamps were on the floor and the side tables between the beds. Two men sat facing piles of nickels, dimes, and quarters.

"Nickel a game," said the other man. "You in?"

"Is everything to your satisfaction?" a steward bellowed as he hammered on the door.

"Nah," the man shuffling the deck of cards yelled. "The crew bangs on the doors."

Jack smiled at his heavy sarcasm. "You know those guys are going to make our beds," he said as he pulled up a chair and sat on it backwards. "This is how fancy people travel to Europe."

"That's because they haven't converted these babies to warships yet," the card dealer said. "All they've done is paint out the identification marks."

The sleek looking man with dark hair curling out through his open shirt had black oval eyes and hooded lids. "My name's Billington," he said to Richard. "Ted Billington."

Jack jerked his thumb at the man next to him "This is Charlie McAllister, but he goes by his nickname, Swipes."

The six-foot man, shrivelled by sun and tobacco, gave Richard a crooked smile. His red-rimmed watery eyes sat above a long bony nose. His long limbs and ginger hair reminded Richard of one of Mr. Vogel's rusted rakes.

Swipes tapped the side of his nose. "If you ever need anything," he said, "just ask. I specialize in knowing helpful people." He folded a stick of gum into his mouth and smiled.

"I guess this is a once in a lifetime trip," Richard said, leaning against the wall to watch.

"Enjoy it," Ted told them all. "It's not every day we rankers get to travel like officers."

Richard watched Ted sort his cards into order. "I think I'll say goodbye to the shore," he said, moving towards the door.

"Don't get lost," Jack called out behind him.

Before the door latch caught, Richard overheard their comments.

"Maybe we should have asked him to play Parcheesi."

"When did they start signing up kids?"

"He came up from signal camp," Jack said. "He wouldn't have been there if he wasn't old enough."

Richard slipped past the blackout door on to the deck. He leaned on the rail watching the last bits of land disappear as the other great ships surged alongside. He was on his way.

◆

"Every soldier is allowed a certain number of days leave during the course of a year," the battery commander told them the night of their first lecture in the ship's lounge. "A railway warrant is issued for travel every six months. But it's not for sale. If caught at this game, you can expect trouble."

Richard raised his brows. *What kind of soldier would do that?*

"While on board," the major thundered, "you don't have to salute every time you see the same officer." He paced up and down the aisles of folding chairs speaking in a clipped voice. "Pay your respects in the morning and when you go off duty."

Ted leaned across Richard and said to Swipes, "We may forget how."

Jack had to cover his mouth with his hand to suppress laughter.

The major shot the four of them a look.

After the lecture, they walked to the dining room where each table held a stack of bingo cards and a bucket of paper squares. Ted and Swipes, preferring card games in their own cabin, left. A sing-along, led by an auxiliary services officer, followed the game of bingo.

"Don't know about you," Jack said, as they headed back to their cabin. "If I have to hear 'Home on the Range' every night, I'll look forward to hearing a discouraging word."

———◆———

Jack's mutterings while he put on his boots the next morning woke Richard. "At least there's only one general parade," he said.

Richard smiled as he remembered Amy's reaction to the word "parade" when he'd told her about summer camp. "How exciting," she'd said, clapping her hands. "Last time I saw a parade was on Dominion Day, but there were only a couple of floats and no elephants at all."

"It's not that kind of parade," he'd explained. "That's the word for inspection."

Jack continued their conversation. "Duties on a ship should belong to the navy."

"Tell that to the sergeant major," Richard said, sitting up. "What did you pull?"

"It's not so bad," Jack confessed. "I'm not peeling spuds or washing pots," he said as he combed his hair and straightened his shirt. "Two hours in the canteen, probably counting chocolate bars."

The army posted weekly orders detailing the duties. No one escaped. Richard remembered Mr. Black's advice. "The sergeant major just loves giving out extra duties. Show up, do your best, and leave. Never look idle or they'll find something else for you to do. If you squawk you get extra. If you complain about extra duty you get even more."

Richard ripped back his bed covers and hopped out of bed. He had pulled the same two duties every day. He was to sweep the passageway and act as spare signaller on the bridge.

In the dining room a gold menu with a tasselled cord down the middle listed the courses to be served for breakfast. Jugs of orange juice and carafes of coffee waited for the soldiers on tables set with silverware and china. The waiters, in starched white jackets and spotless gloves, lifted silver covers to reveal crisp bacon, fluffy scrambled eggs, and slices of toast.

After breakfast, Richard reported to the bridge.

"Name's Willie," the tough little sailor said, sticking out his hand. He smelled of wet wool and liniment. Rimless glasses sat slightly below his beady brown eyes.

Richard shook his hand. "I'm Richard."

"They call me a Liver-Puddlian," Willie said. "Where do you hail from?"

"Well," Richard said with a smile. "I guess I'm a kind of 'puddlian' too. I come from Niagara Falls. Ever heard of it?"

The man threw back his head and roared with laughter. "That's some puddle alright."

He held out a clipboard with a pen attached by a piece of wire. "Messages are sent from one ship to another by lamp in Morse code," Willie explained. "You're to write as I read." His eyes raked Richard from top to toe. "You sure you know how to do this?"

Richard ignored the question, having heard it so often before, and took the clipboard. "Good enough to give you some time off," he said. He knew the idea of getting a break would appeal to the seasoned sailor. Richard watched the old guy's mouth twitch at the corners when he said, "That was part four of my training."

Willie's features crinkled into a wry smile. He took a small, flat silver case from his pocket and with stained yellow fingers extracted a cigarette. "There's the metal key," he indicated with a slant of his head. Then he smiled as he left Richard watching the water.

CHAPTER 11

Lord Haw-Haw

Since there was no room for route marches, after duty the soldiers had the rest of their time free to do as they pleased. Richard spent most of his time on the bridge with Willie. On occasion, Jack joined them.

"How many ships are there in this convoy?" Jack asked.

"*Empress of Australia*, *Monarch of Bermuda*, *Aquitaine*, and *Duchess of Bedford* are all carrying troops," Willie answered. "The *Resolution* and the other destroyers are just along for the ride."

"They're most likely looking for U-boats," Jack said with a grimace as Willie moved to the grey metal wall of dials and knobs. The stuttering of the wireless band crackled into the room.

"What are you putting on?" Richard asked.

"Sometimes we get music on a foreign broadcast," Willie replied.

To Richard's and Jack's surprise, the clear sounds of an aristocratic English announcer came through. As he spoke, Richard could picture a man with a long nose, wearing a monocle over one eye and a gardenia in his buttonhole.

"Germany calling, Germany calling from Hamburg on Brennen and DBX on the 31 meter shortwave band," the Englishman said.

"What did that guy just say?" Richard asked as he stepped closer to the speaker. "He said something about Germany."

"You are about to hear the German news in English," the elegant voice informed them.

Richard and Jack sat down to listen.

The radio voice spoke once again in an exaggerated English drawl. "Germany has solved problems the British have not yet started to tackle. Some day their unemployed men, women, boys, and girls will call their government to account."

"Who is this guy?" Richard asked. "He's not supporting the Commonwealth."

"Some think it is either that traitor Norman Baillie-Stewart," Willie told him, "or Dr. Helmut Hoffman. He used to lecture on Nazism in Scotland." He turned up the dial. "Most Britons refer to him as Lord Haw-Haw."

"Lord Haw-Haw," both Richard and Jack repeated in amazement.

"It's because he gives us all a good laugh."

"We are at war," the voice informed them. "A war the British have brought about in the name of all those virtues which they have failed to practice. It is now time to speak openly of these hypocrisies which previously did not concern us."

"It's nothing but Nazi propaganda," Willie explained.

"Here is the first news bulletin of the day," voice said. "A German U-boat has sunk one of Britain's largest merchant ships, the *Empress of Britain*."

"That's us!" Richard said, leaping up from his chair.

Jack grabbed the field glasses and ran to the window. "I don't see anything."

"Don't pay any attention," Willie told them.

"Britain, your naval prestige is being destroyed," the upper-crust voice said. "We Germans command the seas."

"It won't be the last of the false reports of the good old *Empress*," Willie told them both. "According to the Germans, she'll be sunk a dozen more times before this war is done."

Richard headed back to his cabin, took off his boots, and stretched out on the bed.

———◆———

The quartermaster pushed open the cabin door and tossed Richard a letter. "First and last one I ever hand deliver," he said with a smile. "It's from the bag that came on board. There won't be any more mail for a good while."

The postmark was from Niagara Falls. Richard recognized the large loopy letters. He flipped open his antler-handled pocket-knife, slit the envelope, and removed a sheet of creamy linen-like stationery.

Dear Richard,

How are you? I am writing to tell you about your mother.

Richard's heart stopped. *What if* … He looked about the room in panic. If the news was bad he had no way of getting back home. He made himself read on.

> She is the ONLY one on the street that
> has not joined the Ladies' Auxiliary.

Richard smiled. He had forgotten about Amy's way of thinking. Everything was dramatic.

> It meets once a month at Mrs. Black's house.
> Of course my mother got a headache just
> before it started and she stayed home. Mrs.
> Black served cookies and I poured tea. We
> learned how to wash the label off of our tin
> cans, put the top and the bottom lids inside,
> flatten it with our feet, and save it for collec-
> tion. They also talked about raising money
> for our boys overseas. When I asked about
> the men, they laughed. This month we are
> knitting socks. I have to guess at your size
> because I am NOT GOING TO TALK TO
> YOUR MOTHER.

Richard lifted his foot and appraised the toe of his sock. He'd be happy with a new pair.

> I heard Mrs. B. tell Mr. B. you left because
> he filled your head with army nonsense.
> Our third housekeeper quit and went
> to Toronto. My mother told me to put
> another ad in the paper for a new one.
> This time I'm going to say the person who
> takes the job gets to wear my mother's fur
> coat once a week.

Bye,
Amy

Richard folded the letter with a grin, but it soon faded. *What if people at home heard that Haw-Haw broadcast?* he thought.

He hopped off the bed and padded down the hall to the card game. Jack was in the middle of imitating Lord Haw-Haw.

"What about the people that think the reports are for real?" Richard asked.

"Someone from the war office will pass word along that it's false," Ted said. "Although, there are a few women I know that wouldn't regret the news."

"Left a few wives behind, did you?" Swipes teased.

"More than a few," Ted said with a smile.

All Richard could think of was Mr. and Mrs. Black settling with their cup of tea in front of the radio at six o'clock. He prayed the McLaughlin radio crackled loudly that night and his mother had hers off as usual.

CHAPTER 12

Aldershot

After several weeks at sea, finally skirting Greenland, the Canadian troops looked forward to setting foot on dry land before the end of the year. Richard watched the great ocean liners crowd into the British harbour from the ship's bridge.

"So where exactly are we?" Jack asked, coming to his side.

"We cast anchor off Gourock in the Firth of Clyde," Richard answered. He had asked Willie that very question as he watched him cross off the number seventeen on his December calendar on the back of the door.

"The fifth of Clyde?" Jack asked. "They got a different kind of calendar over here?"

"Firth," Richard corrected, "is another word for river."

Thousands of people waited on the platform to greet them as their train pulled into the Glasgow Station. Jack caught a small packet tossed from the crowd. "They're throwing us food," he said with a grin. "I just caught a sandwich."

"Let's throw them something back," Richard said. He pulled out his pocket change and threw his Canadian coins into the cheering crowd. Soon the rest were doing the same.

"Big commotion over nothing," Ted said. "This thing will be over in a year."

"Next stop, Aldershot," roared the voices of the commanding officers down the line.

"Would you look at the size of that train?" Jack yelled above the din when the tiny London and South West Railway engine pulled into the station. Its whistle sounded like the screech of an angry cat.

"I've seen bigger ones going around a Christmas tree," Swipes said, making them laugh.

With packs on backs, ammunition pouches across the front, haversacks on the right, and water bottle and bayonet on the left, only eight men could squeeze into a tiny carriage.

As they passed the miles of tilled farmland, the old inns and countryside homes fascinated Richard, but not the others. All they wanted to do was play cards. Within hours they pulled to a stop along a siding. Tins of corned beef and hard biscuits made their way through the train.

Willie was right, Richard thought. *No trains travel at night; the lights are too easily spotted by the Luftwaffe.* He removed his gear and settled himself in the corridor for a bite to eat, happy to hide from Germany's air force, one of the strongest in the world.

"Eating from a tin, while we sit in a tin," Jack commented.

"So what are we?" someone asked as the sun went down. "Sardines or oysters?"

"The pearl in the oyster is gone," Ted said. "Point is not to end up fish bait."

The next morning Fleet Station appeared on the west side of a stone bridge. The road from the station lay quiet.

"His peach fuzz hasn't even come in yet," Swipes said, remarking on Richard's fresh morning face. Unlike the others, he didn't have the dark shadow of an unshaven soldier.

"You sure you ain't a girl?" Ted asked.

"I thought it did nothing but rain in England," Jack said to Richard when they got off.

"That's what I heard too," Richard said, taking a look at the morning sky. Not a sign of a snowflake or icy raindrop. It was as if they had September weather for Christmas.

"So what's with the drought?" Jack asked, pointing to the sign.

Fleet Pond was nothing but a huge hole beside the road.

The troop marched without speaking, their belts, buckles, and badges gleaming in the sun. Richard spotted two young boys behind a road block and gave them a wink. They saluted him.

When they broke rank at the camp gate, everyone's eyes widened. Leipzig barracks, their new home, had been built during the Boer War at the turn of the century.

Ted said what most of them had on their mind. "And we thought the train was a joke."

"As long as we don't have to sleep in there," Jack commented as they walked past the many rows of horse stalls.

Richard stepped away from the unit into the cool interior of the stalls. The smell of horses took him back to Mr. Vogel's barn where he eased the horse from the rig. Richard loved unbuckling the belly band, taking off his harness and hanging it up. First he'd rub the place on the horse's back and neck where they had chafed. Then he unclipped the reins, undid the bridle, and took the bit from the horse's mouth. As Richard's eyes adjusted to the dim light, the reality of where he was returned.

The officers behind the barb-wired gate checked them in and pointed to the table piled with blankets, barrack bags, and other equipment. The huts that waited for them at the end of their march weren't much better than the stables. The walls and roofs were wooden. The crude central heating system of small open grates shocked them all.

"No hot water," Swipes called out from the back, "and the cold faucet drips."

"We'll have it fixed up in no time," one of the officers said. "Those with a trade report directly to the quartermaster. Sawmill in town does all kinds of work for the army."

"Let me get this straight," Ted said, once the officer was out of earshot. "We came all this way to renovate?"

Richard, Jack, Ted, and Swipes were assigned to the same hut. No sooner had he dumped his gear than Swipes disappeared. It was well after midnight before he slid back inside.

Battle drill began the next morning. Richard learned to march in right flank, pincer attack, and frontal attack formations. Next, they practiced getting over and around anything they would encounter on a battlefield. Richard trod through cow dung, scaled hills and climbed trees with more ease than the rest, but by the end of the day, he was just as exhausted.

Dear Mr. Black,

I am writing this from a small hut with three other guys. We marched all the way from the railway station. One of the guy's names is Charlie, but everyone calls him Swipes. Jack and a guy named Ted are both from St. Catharines.

Right now our real quarters are nothing more than concrete foundations. We've got to build them ourselves from the base up. There's even a rumour that they expect the Canadians to build an airfield.

Now I know what you meant when you used to say how a blanket and a pair of dry socks felt like heaven. Last night we slept in full battledress just to stay warm. Tell Amy I'm looking forward to my new wool socks.

Richard

Richard woke to a shake and the sound of rain leaking through their dingy hut.

"Get up," Swipes whispered into his ear.

Richard rolled over, having no intention of participating in a card game at this time of night. But Swipes wouldn't let him rest.

"Aren't you tired of being grubby," he said, shaking Richard's shoulder. "Jack," he called out in a hoarse whisper. "Don't you want hot water?"

They trailed after Swipes in the dark.

"This place is out of bounds," Jack hissed. "It's army headquarters."

"So we pull it into bounds," Swipes replied.

"Pull what?" Jack asked.

Swipes pointed to the large semi-trailer truck on wheels, parked under a tree. "It's the mobile laundry unit," he said, "with a boiler to heat water. All we got to do is hook it up."

"Put her in gear," Ted directed. "We'll push."

Swipes jumped behind the wheel.

Richard stood in the dark, unsure of what to do. Mr. Black had never told him anything about this kind of army activity.

"Come on, kid," Ted said, smacking him on the back. "You must want a hot bath."

Richard, Jack, and Ted pushed, while Swipes steered it to the field behind the huts.

"What about the guard?' Richard whispered.

"He'll want a bath too," Ted replied. "Unhook those hoses and start the generator."

As soon as the machine was set up, Jack stripped off his clothes and jumped into the large metal tub.

"Wait," Richard cried, who understood something Jack didn't, having watched his mother's laundry business. But it was too late.

84

"Ahhh!" Jack yelled when the freezing water hit.

Richard clapped his hand across his forehead. "I knew the first rinse would be cold."

The tub drained and refilled. This time the water was hot. Richard, Swipes, and Ted stripped and climbed in. They sloshed the deliciously hot water over their bodies.

"What about towels?" Ted asked.

Richard looked about. "Tumble driers," he said. "My mother always wanted one."

"You want us to get inside?" Swipes asked in amazement. "No thanks."

"Just unhook the hose," Richard said.

Swipes rifled through the piles of clothes and produced four sets of clean underwear and socks. He tossed them to the men drying themselves in the stream of hot air from the hoses.

They all stopped dressing at the sound of the rap on the door.

"You guys done yet?" the duty guard whispered.

Jack, dressed first, took the guard's rifle and helmet. He raced into position with the tongue of his boots flapping.

The soap, clean underwear, and socks helped Richard get over his guilty feelings as he made his way back to the hut. By the time the sun came up, a new guard was in place, the laundry unit was back at headquarters, and the four gunners sat at the foot of their beds polishing their boots.

The sergeant stuck his head into the hut. "Inspection," he shouted, jolting them into smoothing down the blankets and standing tall in front of them.

Colonel Cuddles' real name was Campbell, but the large jowls on either side of his soft round face reminded everyone of a big baby in uniform. He stopped in front of each of the men and looked them over. When he got to Richard, he removed his hat and placed it under his arm. "I hear you do well at signalling," the colonel commented.

Richard's eyes shifted from the shiny buckle on the officer's belt to the gleaming badge on his peaked cap. "Thank you sir," he replied.

"Can you ride?" the colonel asked.

"A horse?" was all Richard could think of saying.

The colonel's eyes cooled as he turned to the officer beside him. "This soldier does know that he is in the artillery?" he asked.

Ted and Swipes snickered.

He turned back to Richard. "A motorcycle, soldier," he said. "Can you ride a bike?"

"Yes sir," Richard replied with a face as red as a beet. "I trained at Camp Niagara, sir."

The colonel turned and left the tent. Richard sank to his cot in complete embarrassment.

"Something's up," Ted commented.

CHAPTER 13

Mail

"Mail call," a soldier called into the doorway of their hut. "Report to the Q.M."

Everyone pulled on their boots.

"Aren't you coming?" Richard asked Swipes, who remained lounging on his cot.

"I'll be along," he said. "It's a pain to have to wait for them to sort it."

"At least your name doesn't start with a Y," Richard replied with a smile.

Ted Billington and Jack Gill had received a handful of letters and a couple of parcels when Swipes finally arrived at the quartermaster's. "I just hope someone sent me a loaf of bread," he said with impatience.

"Bread?" Jack repeated, sorting through his mail. "Wouldn't it be stale by now?"

"Especially if it came with this lot," Richard said, showing them the words "salvaged from the sea" stamped across the back of his only envelope.

"Won't matter," Swipes said. "It's what's inside that counts."

"So what do you think happened to the ship?" Richard asked as he stared at the water-stained corner of his letter.

"Probably caught a torpedo or ran into a mine," Swipes said.

Richard gave a silent prayer that it wasn't the *Empress* and that Willie was safe.

Back at their hut, Jack spread the soap, chocolate bars, and packages of cigarettes that came from his parcel across his bed. He wound a knitted scarf around his neck. "Hey Richard," he said, tossing him a Sweet Marie. "Put this in your pocket. You just never know when it will come in handy."

Ted pulled out socks, cigarettes, and a couple of magazines that went under his pillow.

Swipes entered the hut.

"Get your loaf of bread?" they all asked at once.

"Yup," Swipes said to their puzzled faces. And to their surprise, he pulled a much battered, sickly green loaf out of a long cardboard box.

"I thought you were kidding," Richard said as he moved closer for a better look at the moldy green object. "I don't think that's safe to eat."

"I don't plan to eat it," Swipes said. He sliced off the crust with his bayonet and reached inside. "I plan to drink it," he said, pulling out a bottle of whiskey.

Richard and Jack looked at each other and chuckled. Their chuckles turned to belly-laughs. Richard laughed so hard he lay on the floor holding his stomach.

When it was over, he crawled on to his cot and used the corner of his grey army blanket to wipe his eyes. Happy to see Amy's familiar fat round letters dotted with small circles and crossed with bow ties, he opened his mail.

Dear Richard,

How are you? I spent most of last night
rolling bandages for the Red Cross.

    I want to tell you that there are a lot
of strange things happening in this town.
There is a sign in the window of Mr.
Collin's Bookstore that says THERE'S A
WAR GOING ON AND I'VE GONE TO
SEE WHAT ITS ALL ABOUT. I thought
Mr. Collins was a smart man, having all
those books around him. Why didn't he
know what the war is all about? Then
Mr. Lee put a sign in the window of his
laundry WILL CLEAN SHIRTS AFTER
CLEANING AXIS. Why would he go
somewhere else to clean axle grease?

Richard put the letter on his lap and gave another
chuckle. Amy could always make him laugh, pretending
not to read between the lines.

YOUR MOTHER came to visit my father.
He was waiting for her in his study and
closed the door so we couldn't hear. On
the way out I asked her if she thought you
would be visiting relatives while you were
in England. She said why on earth would
he go to Plumstead? The next day Tommy
had to take an envelope to her. He said the
house looked different so I went to sneak

a peek for myself. There was no laundry
anywhere. The dining room table was set
up with all its chairs, but no flowers in the
middle, like at our place.

Richard lowered the letter. *Why had his mother gone to
see Mr. McLaughlin? What was in the envelope? Why was
there no laundry?*

Thoughts bounced about his head.

*Maybe, with the war on, people weren't taking hol-
idays*, he reasoned. *The hotels would be almost empty.
His mother must have lost her job! She probably went to
see Mr. McLaughlin about money. But Grace Fuller would
never take out a loan.* Then the worst thought in the world
entered his mind. *His mother was planning to sell the house.*

Richard closed his eyes and transported himself back
to the fort in the cherry tree. He could almost hear the
rustle of the leaves. He put his head in his hands.

"Bad news?" asked Jack. "Is everything okay?"

Richard raised his head. "It looks like my mother is a
little short of cash."

"Nothing new about that," Swipes commented. But
seeing the look on Richard's face his tone softened. "Go
have a chat with the paymaster. You can send her some of
your pay."

Richard turned the letter over and read on.

Mr. Black brought home this strange stuff
called margarine. They are going to try and
use it until butter comes back. Doesn't that
sound funny? It's like butter just walked

down the street saying it won't come back until the war is over. It is really white lard in a plastic pillow. There is a button of orange liquid in the center. He showed us how to press down on the button to push out the colour. The four of us sat on the porch, passing it around. Each of us took a turn at pressing. Then we made a game of it by tossing it back and forth until it began to look like butter. I took some home but Mother won't eat it. She said I made the whole house smell of greasy lard and went to bed.

Tommy saw Mr. Vogel coming out of the bank and he said hello. Mr. Vogel told him to go away and leave him alone. Tommy said Mr. Vogel is nothing but a DP. What's that?

Did you like your Christmas socks? Mr. Black laughed at the red and green stripes but he said you'd be grateful for them no matter what colour they were.

Write back soon,
Amy

Richard folded the letter and stuffed it back into its envelope. His Christmas socks were probably floating about the ocean. He left the hut to seek out the paymaster, and, after signing a few papers, returned. Richard pulled out his pen and paper and began a letter to his mother, knowing he had to be careful with what he wrote. She didn't like anyone knowing her business.

> Dear Mother,
>
> We are very busy training here in England. The weather is either wet or cold. We only had one day of frost. I wish we had just a little snow, the kind for making snowballs.

He paused to think about Mr. Vogel's field when the snow lay deep in the wheel ruts and the trees bent with the weight of crystal ice.

> I have made arrangements for part of my pay to come home to you. I am making this letter short because I want to get it in tonight's mail bag.
>
> Your son,
> Richard

He stuck the bright red square with the cameo of King George on to the top right hand corner of the envelope and went back out to post it.

CHAPTER 14

Plumstead

Half the regiment would get leave over Christmas, the sign on the notice board read, the other half at New Year. Richard sighed at the thought of Christmas away from home. Mr. and Mrs. Black always put up a Christmas tree even though they didn't have any kids. Tommy and Amy always gave him a present. A lump formed in his throat. His mother would be alone over the holidays.

"Looks like we've both got Christmas leave," Jack said, reading his name from the list over Richard's shoulder. "Why don't you come with me? At least you'll get to see good old London Town."

"Genuine business has come to a stand-still in London," one of the other soldiers from behind said in a fake aristocratic voice, imitating Lord Haw-Haw.

"Well, then," Jack said, thumping Richard on the back, "we better get it going again."

The battery sergeant major looked them over briefly. "I am cautioning you to behave yourself in this country," he said. "Remember the rules about rail passes." He stamped two with the date and pushed them forward. Then he handed each of them a five pound note and a ration card.

"So what's this worth?" Richard asked Jack, as he pocketed the money.

"They've given us a pound a day," Jack said with a large grin. "A British soldier only draws a shilling a day. We're rich!"

A civilian truck took them to the rail station where they boarded the train to London. There they emerged into a thick, dense fog that smelled of grime, cement, and wet burned wood.

"Don't know about you," Jack said. "I don't want to have to find my way about in this blackout. Let's find the serviceman's club. It'll only be sixpence for the night. Tomorrow we can paint the town red."

Richard followed Jack like a lost puppy to a club in a basement off an alley. Inside the thick stone walls a sailor played an upright piano. The buzz of conversation and the smell of bacon and beans filled the warm, noisy room. Servicemen of every kind sat at small varnished tables, topped with a single candle and a jar of change. Richard and Jack waded their way through thick tobacco smoke to a table that had a teapot, a bowl of sugar, small bottle of milk, several mugs, and a basket of digestive cookies.

"Just throw your loose change in the jar, and then help yourself," Jack told him. "There are no fixed prices, unless you order."

As Richard fished for a few coins from his trouser pocket, the air raid siren went off. He stopped and stared up at the black mildewed ceiling. The men at the next table waved him to sit down as if it was against the rules to stand. The overhead rumblings made the old foundations shiver. The sailor at the piano banged out a more rousing tune.

Once they got the all clear, Richard and Jack headed off to bed.

The next day, the fog having barely lifted, Jack told Richard of his change in plans. "I think I'll go to look up some of my relatives in Oxford," he said. "You can come along if you want. Maybe we'll get a Christmas dinner."

Long-lost relatives might be better than no family at all, Richard thought. He decided to try his own luck and head for Plumstead.

"A twenty minute train ride," he was told at Waterloo train station. "Just past Woolwich Arsenal."

Richard boarded a train. A Wren in her khaki uniform and snappy little hat, buying a ticket, made him think of Amy.

Upon arrival in Plumstead, Richard headed for the police station.

"Hello, soldier," the policeman behind the desk greeted him. "What can I do for you?"

"I'm not sure if I'm on a wild goose chase," Richard said with a shrug. "I might have some relatives in town. Do you know anyone by the name of William Fuller?"

The desk sergeant leaned across the desk and looked him up and down.

"Richard's boy?" he asked. "I went to school with him, but heard he died."

Richard nodded, unable to speak for the lump in his throat. Meeting someone who had gone to school with his father made his dad somehow all the more real, all the more dead and all the more missed, all at once.

"You're looking for 18 Ceres Road," the policeman said. "It's just off High Street, behind the last church. It's a good long walk."

Richard pushed open the small gate of the low wooden fence at the end of the quiet cul-de-sac and followed the brick path that led to a dark green door. The lace curtains in the front window trembled in the lemon-coloured light of the late afternoon. Just as he was about to knock, the door flew open.

"I've only just got in myself," the pretty, plump woman said, putting her hand to her hair as if to tidy a fresh set. Richard noticed small grey hairs flecking the curly brown hair that framed her round smiling face. "Your Uncle William will be so happy to meet you. I expect the sergeant rang his factory as well," she said. "He'll leave work straight away. If we had known you were coming, we'd have met you at the train."

The pleasant woman took Richard by the arm into a tiny sitting room with a fire blazing behind a shiny black grate. Gleaming brass bells and china dogs stood along the dark mantelpiece. A massive roll-top desk filled most of the room. Newspaper clippings, accounts, bills, registration documents, and letters spilled across it. Beside it sat a basket filled with cloth pieces and a rag rug in process. The air in the house had a strong smell of cooked vegetables and furniture polish.

"Sit, sit. I'm your Auntie Joyce. The police officer rang the rectory," she said, arranging a pillow behind Richard's back. "Everyone knows that's where I am most mornings, being secretary of the parish council, but you can imagine my surprise when the minister came to say the police were on the line for me." Her hands went to her heart. "My first thought was something had happened to William. We are all so jumpy these days what with the war on," she explained. Then she gave a large smile and shook her head. "But why on earth am I telling a soldier there's a war on?"

So overwhelmed by the warm welcome and the news that he had an Aunt Joyce and an Uncle William, all Richard could do was sit and grin. He had no sooner felt the warmth of the fire when the front door banged open. Richard looked up to a much older, much more tired version of his father in a canvas work coat.

"Eh lad," he said, putting his hands on his hips. "You do favour your dad."

Richard rose as the man strode towards him.

The man placed a large calloused hand on his shoulder and pushed him back down. Then he held it out for Richard to shake it. "I'm your Uncle Will," he said. "I've still got the telegram your dad, God rest his soul, sent me the day you were born. I pictured you a bit younger, but here you are, right in front of me, old enough to serve the Commonwealth." He slapped Richard on the back.

"I told him we'd have met him at the train, if we'd known he was coming," Joyce said. "He must have walked all over town."

"Soldiers are used to walking, aren't you, lad?"

Richard nodded, still unable to find his voice.

"Not likely to get a chance to be one, myself," his uncle said. He pulled a chair towards Richard and sat down. "I've got a 'deferred' occupation in the arsenal down the road."

"You'll stay for your tea," said Joyce.

"He'll be staying longer than that, I hope," Will boomed. "How many days leave?"

"Three left," Richard replied.

"Then take off your boots," his uncle told him with a hearty laugh.

Tea turned out to be much more than a cup from a pot. Joyce served him a small piece of fatty beef, potatoes, Brussels sprouts, and a great slab of Yorkshire pudding covered with gravy. Will poured out a shot of whiskey and passed it across the table to him. Richard shook his head in refusal. Will shrugged, took it back, and downed it in one gulp.

After eating, Richard and his uncle retired to the sitting room. From the kitchen came the rattle of cups and tinkle of glass. Will took out an old briar pipe and tattered tobacco pouch from his waistcoat pocket.

"How's your mother?" he asked.

"Fine," Richard said.

"Is she still at the same address?" he asked, packing the pipe with tobacco.

"Yes," Richard said, hoping his statement to be true when he got back.

"Never remarried?"

"Nope," Richard said.

"Fifteen years is a long time to be alone," William said as he reached for the twist of paper that lay across the mantle and held it against the glowing coals until it flamed.

"Longer than that," Richard mumbled, casting his eyes to the ground, hoping to keep up the pretense of his age.

William lit his pipe and sank into one of the overstuffed armchairs. "Your mother certainly won my brother's heart," he said with a great sigh. "He was head over heels in love with her."

"Every girl was in love with Richard," Aunt Joyce added as she rolled in a wooden cart set with a china teapot, matching cups, and a glass cake stand with a clear dome. Under it were three digestive biscuits.

"Except for you," Uncle Will teased.

"Except for me," she repeated as she looked at Richard. "Don't get me wrong, he didn't try to make them fall in love. They just couldn't help it, when they looked into those merry blue eyes beneath that blonde hair." She paused, smiled and said, "Eyes just like yours."

"Do you have a telephone at home?" Will asked.

"No, we don't," Richard responded. He thought of Mrs. Black taking orders on the phone as they spoke. "Family up the street has one, though."

"Damn noisy things," his Uncle Will said. "They go off at all hours in the factory office. You have to shout your head off to make yourself heard."

"Without it, we would have missed his visit," Joyce said handing him a cup and saucer.

"My brother's son wouldn't be the kind of lad that would have only called around once," Will replied. "Isn't that so," he said, his eyes sparkling.

"That's right sir," Richard said, taking his tea from his aunt. "Thanks."

A chunk of soot fell from the chimney into the flames with a thud.

"That chimney needs sweeping," Joyce announced. "I've no idea when it was done last, with all the young lads gone."

Richard put down his cup. "I'll do it for you, Aunt Joyce," he said. "Just put out the dustpan and broom in the morning."

Joyce smiled at him over the rim of the cup then turned to her husband. "On your way to the allotment tomorrow, find me a chimney sweep," she said. She turned to Richard. "I've given you the first room on the left," his aunt said, "and put a pair of wellies by the back door so you don't have to put your boots back on when you pay your visit."

"Our smallest room in the house is in the back garden," Uncle Will said with a wink, "for when you have to see a man about a dog."

The tiny red brick outhouse had a strong box-type seat. A wooden toilet seat covered the large round hole in the centre. A few old magazines sat beside it and roll of paper stuck out from the nail on the wall across from it.

Having no choice, Richard settled himself as best he could and gazed upward. A tin bath hung above his head, suspended by a ceiling rope. Two dining chairs hung from wooden pegs on the wall farther down. The third wooden peg suggested to Richard that the chair he sat on at the table had been there shortly before he arrived. He studied the outdated family portraits on the wall facing him, searching for a family resemblance.

CHAPTER 15

The Aunties

"You take this," Joyce said, handing Richard a wicker basket the next morning after a breakfast of porridge and tea. "William will empty the earth closet. We take everything down to the garden patch at our allotment."

Richard watched his uncle open a small door on the rear wall of the outhouse, pull out a tin bucket, and fasten it with a lid.

"There's not much to see in town," his aunt told him. "You can stay here if you like."

"Don't worry, Auntie Joyce," Richard called back as they headed out the back gate, his uncle carrying the bucket. "It'll be a lot more interesting than being in the barracks."

She smiled and waved her tea towel.

Along the way, Richard's uncle explained. "Every scrap of food goes down that hole, along with tea leaves, sweepings from the floor, lawn clippings, and soot." Richard's eyebrows shot up when he heard him say, "Your aunt even breaks the bones with a hammer."

Their first stop was the village shop. Will left the bucket on the step and pushed open the door. The small brass bell over the frame jingled.

"Good morning, Will," the shopkeeper said, "and you too, soldier."

Richard smiled at the stout man in the green-bibbed apron. His round face, beneath a head of thin blond hair, appeared flushed.

"I heard you were Richard's boy," he said. "I always liked your dad. You know, he never had a bad word to say about anyone." He turned to Will. "Anything in particular?"

"We need a chimney sweep," Will told the shopkeeper as Richard moved to a rack of assorted postcards. "Anyone left in town that can do it?"

"Old Tom Shanks is your man," the shopkeeper told him. "He's out on his rounds just the now. When I see his missus, I'll tell her you need an appointment."

"I'll take this," Richard said, placing the sepia postcard of Plumstead's main street on the counter. He fished into his uniform pocket for some change.

"Can't sell you that I'm afraid," the shopkeeper said.

Richard looked at the man with a puzzled face.

The shopkeeper picked it up and handed it to Richard. "But I can give it to you," he said. "It's the least I can do for a boy who came across the ocean to protect his father's homeland."

"Thanks," Richard said, placing the card in his inner pocket.

"He really does favour his dad," the shopkeeper said to Will as they headed for the door. "Do his aunties know that he is in town?"

"They will," his Uncle Will assured him. "Believe me, they will."

Will took him down the road toward a large country

home, Richard taking his turn at carrying the pail. The ivy-covered stone mansion with a blue slate roof overlooked sweeping well-kept lawns. A formal front garden of interestingly shaped shrubs separated the house from the road.

"Nice place," Richard commented as they made their way to the back of the estate. To his surprise, the vast back lawn was nothing more than a small central patch of withered grass. The owner had divided his entire property into rectangular garden plots.

Clumps of harvested parsnips and stalks of Brussels sprouts lay on top of Will's rectangular patch of soil. He tossed a few vegetables into the basket.

"Won't they freeze like that?" Richard asked.

"The frost sweetens them," Uncle Will replied. "Everyone will pick up a few for their Christmas dinner."

"Who is everyone?" Richard asked.

"Everyone in the allotment," Uncle Will explained, as he emptied the contents of the covered pail into a small wooden box. "We all share."

"Are there chickens in there?" Richard asked, as he pointed to a small brick house surrounded by cement blocks.

"We are when we go in," Will said with a hearty laugh. "That's the estate bomb shelter."

Richard looked up at the cold blue sky. He had forgotten about the Luftwaffe.

Will pointed to one of the wooden sheds across the way. "One fella uses that to raise rabbits. We've eaten so many rabbits this year, every time a dog barks we run."

Richard grinned and sauntered over to have a look at the pens.

"The owner lets everyone help themselves to wind-falls," William said, picking a few small apples from the ground around the bordering orchard. "This is a Cox's Orange Pippin," he said. "They don't keep past December. Most people celebrate Christmas with an apple tart."

Our apples are so much bigger, Richard thought. *Everything in Canada seems to be bigger than it is in England. Cars are bigger, milk bottles are bigger, even the robins are bigger.* It made him wonder why Hitler was going to invade England instead of Canada.

"Have you a garden at home?" Will asked.

"Not really," Richard said. He didn't want to explain that their backyard held nothing but clothes lines. *It would be a good place for a rabbit hutch,* he thought. *It wouldn't take much to build one. There's still wood from Mr. Black's garage and it wouldn't be hard to find an old piece of screen-ing.* They wouldn't eat the rabbits though, Amy would have a fit.

"We've got a cherry tree," Richard said, continuing the conversation.

"Good tasting?"

"You bet," Richard said. "Best Bings on the street."

❖

"We're in the dining room," Joyce called out on their return. "Have a good wash."

Joyce sat at the table with two women as thin as knitting needles in matching pink cardigans and pearl necklaces. Both had brown hair, pale complexions, and gold spectacles over brown eyes.

One appeared as fussy as old hen, straightening the buttons of her sweater and adjusting the cuffs of her blouse.

The black bobby pins on the sides of the other's head gave her look of a little girl.

"Hello Edith," Will boomed out, extending his hand, "or is it Emily?"

The woman smiled. "You are correct," she said in a prim voice. "I am Edith."

Her twin peeked at Richard over the edge of the lace handkerchief she held to her nose.

Will drew Richard forward. "Let me introduce you, lad," he said. "This is your Aunt Edith and your Aunt Emily, on your mother's side."

"That would make you my mother's sisters," Richard said, extending his hand to Edith. "I am pleased to meet you."

Edith shook his hand.

Emily waved her fingers as her handkerchief inched up to her lower lashes.

"Handsome, isn't he?" Will said, giving Richard such a great slap on the back, he fell into his seat. "We've brought everyone parsnips and Brussels sprouts."

"Thank you," Edith said, with a small upward nod of approval. She took a delicate sip from her china cup. "I suppose you expect us to invite you for Christmas dinner, Richard."

Before Richard could answer, Joyce passed him a plate of treacled bread. "I was thinking of having you and Emily here for dinner," she said with a smile. "That way we could all enjoy his company. What do you think, Richard?"

"Is there a restaurant in town?" Richard asked.

"Only one," William said, "along with a few cafes. Why?"

Richard reached into his pocket, pulled out the remainder of his five pounds and his ration card, and spread it all out in front of them. "Let me treat all of you to Christmas dinner," he said.

"I wouldn't hear of it," Joyce said, bringing her teacup down with a clunk. "Edith, bring along what you have and we'll cobble it all together."

Emily lowered her handkerchief into her lap. She reached across the table and pushed the coins off of the pound notes. "There is the pantomime," she said, turning to Edith.

"My sister prefers to spend money on something frivolous like a pantomime or the cinema," Edith said, with a roll of her eyes.

Emily looked a Richard and blinked. "Edith would buy a book instead of a loaf of bread."

"Do you read, Richard?" Edith asked.

He thought for a minute. "I read *The Wizard of Oz*."

Edith lifted her brows to her hairline and looked at her sister. Richard knew it was the signal for a poor excuse for a book.

"A friend of mine gave it to me," he added in defense.

"Your mother wasn't much of a reader," Edith said, "but she was good at numbers." She looked at Joyce and sniffed. "I can't imagine spending my life with someone who didn't read."

Richard's Aunt Joyce fixed a smile to her face and put down her cup. "Did you find any windfalls for chutney?" she asked her husband.

"Chutney," Richard repeated. "What's that?"

"Chutney," Edith stated, as if she were dictating a lesson, "is a relish made from fruit, spices, sugar, and vinegar."

"I love strawberry jam, especially on scones with clotted cream," Emily said, tilting her head from one side to the other as she spoke. "It's been so long since we've had clotted cream."

"What's a pantomime?" Richard asked. *There are so many different words used in Britain,* he thought, *even though they speak English.*

His Aunt Edith gave out an exaggerated sigh. "It is a style of British theatre traditionally performed at Christmas, in which a children's story is told in song and dance."

Richard turned to his other aunt. "Aunt Emily," he asked, "what is the story this year?"

Emily gave a clap using the tips of her fingers. "This year it's Dick Whittington." Then she placed her fingers on her heart. "I do love that story. I read it the day your father brought your mother lilies."

"The day our father insisted he state his intentions," Edith said, "or stop coming round."

"It is my entire fault," Emily said placing her long, thin fingers on either side of her face and staring down into her teacup. "I told her eloping was so romantic."

"They married in the country church," Edith said, frowning at her sister.

"She sailed away and was gone forever," Emily said. "We thought an animal had eaten her!"

"Grace stopped writing after Richard died," Edith said, wagging her finger at Edith.

"So wild out there in Canada," Emily said. "Do you live in a cabin?"

"Not really," Richard said. "We have a two-storey house with a large kitchen."

"Your earth closet is near the back door, I presume, because of the cold?" Edith asked with a small sniff.

"Our bathroom?" Richard replied. "It's upstairs on the main landing, right across from the spare bedroom. My mother has the back bedroom, I have the front one, and there's one spare."

"Who in their right mind would want such a mucky thing in the house?" Edith asked.

"Grace always had such daring behaviour," Emily said.

"It would be like keeping one's manure heap in the living room," Edith said.

"Or hens in the bedroom," her twin chimed in.

"It's a flush toilet," Richard explained with a shake of his head.

"I wouldn't mind our outhouse being converted," Joyce said to William.

"But, inside the house?" Edith exclaimed in amazement.

"There are indoor water closets everywhere these days," William informed them.

Richard sat back and smiled. They could argue this point until the cows came home but it wouldn't make any difference. Richard recognized this kind of steel-trap mind. *Must run in the family,* he thought.

"After the war you should all come to Canada and see for yourselves."

"I'm afraid the only travelling I will be doing is through books," Edith said.

"I'd love to roam the Canadian mountains, collecting

birds' eggs," Emily said, tapping the tips of her fingers together again in quiet applause.

"Forgetting the edge and falling to your death below," Edith added.

"So what are we going to do about this cat?" Will asked them all in exasperation.

"What cat?" Richard asked.

"Dick Whittington's," everyone chorused.

Richard pushed the small pile of money towards his uncle. "Buy the tickets," he said as all three aunts lifted their cups to sip.

CHAPTER 16

The Truck

Dear Amy,

I had a five day leave. I went to Plumstead, the place on this postcard, to visit my relatives and saw a show. Tell Tommy DP means displaced person and it's disrespectful. Tommy is old enough to work. He should go to Mr. Vogel's farm and help out.

You said you mailed a parcel, but I haven't got it yet. Did you know they measure the mail for the forces by the ton? Looking forward to my new pair of socks.

Richard

◆

Richard took an early morning walk at the end of his night's responsibilities in order to get away from the sprawling complex of red and yellow brick buildings, parade squares, and tents. Night duties weren't all that bad. His meals were brought to the guard house, and even though no one was supposed to sleep, everyone managed to catch a few winks, thanks to an arrangement with the other signaller at headquarters. He always tipped them off when the orderly officer made his rounds, claiming it avoided embarrassment, but Richard knew it was just another example of how soldiers looked out for each other.

In the early morning the Fleet Road hadn't yet filled with its usual traffic of tanks, cars, and trucks. In the silence of the rain-washed morning, he heard the clatter of cart wheels come up behind him.

Richard stopped, turned, and waved.

The stocky farmer had a square weathered face with cheeks that shone like leather. "Morning soldier," he said. "Going anywhere in particular?"

"Just learning the lay of the land," Richard replied. He walked to the front of the cart and patted the golden horse's blonde mane. "What's her name?"

"Treacle," the farmer replied. He lifted a rein and pointed to the yellow-and-green five-ton truck that passed them. "Unlike a truck, you can talk to a horse."

The truck swerved sloppily onto the grassy verge. Richard had noticed Swipes behind the wheel with Ted in the cab, learning to drive on the opposite side of the road.

"Gotta be capable of controlling summat as heavy as that," the farmer said. A dark grey working jacket covered his thick collarless shirt. Letting loose the reins, he took a pipe and tobacco pouch from his waistcoat pocket. The farmer packed the pipe, struck a match on the sole of his shoe and lit it. When he drew on the pipe, twirls of smoke rose above his head.

"My name's Harold, Harold Redfield. You must be one of those Maple Leaf Men."

"Richard Fuller from Niagara Falls," Richard said to the man with the cheerful face. The farmer's flat cap looked as if he had worn it for decades. "That's in Ontario."

"I saw your sad-looking Honeymoon Bridge in the newsreel," the farmer said. "Hop aboard, soldier, I'll give you a tour along the way."

The man jerked the reins and they bumped along the dirt road until they joined the main route into town. "Who would have thought that river ice could bring down a bridge that size," the farmer said, as the village women drew aside their blackout curtains and picked up bottles of milk from their stone steps.

"Worst ice jam in thirty years," Richard said. "It climbed seventy-five feet up the bank."

Harold nodded to the neighbours gossiping on their front walks as they passed. "I miss the ice," he said, "never thought the war would take ours away."

"What do you mean?" Richard asked with interest.

"Fleet Pond," the farmer said. "In winter, when the pond was frozen, everyone went out to skate or watch a game of curling. We used to park a few cars on the road and play until midnight in the headlights."

"At home we don't have to cover the headlights," Richard said.

"Oh, it had nothing to do with the headlights," the farmer told him. "Once those German aircraft started passing overhead to bomb the north, we figured it was too good a landmark on a moonlit night. The village voted to drain the pond."

Richard stared ahead, thinking about the enemy. The people of Fleet could end up under heavy attack, being so close to all the barracks. A cold chill went down his spine. His aunt and uncle lived next door to the Woolich Arsenal in Plumstead.

"You'll have no trouble finding your way about town," Harold told him. "The man who built this town laid the roads out American style. Main roads run parallel to one and another and the other roads intersect."

As they entered the village, bagged lampposts marked the main crossroads. Richard spotted the yellow-and-green truck that Swipes was driving turning down a street.

"Here's the bank," Harold said, pointing to the building with the heavy white-pillared entrance. The windows were behind a wall of sandbags. "Across is the police station."

They clopped along the road as Harold pointed out the fish and chips shop, barber shop, and ironmonger. All the shop windows were cross-hatched with strips of tape to prevent shattering. "That's The Oat Sheaf, the local pub," he said, raising the rein. "But I'll show you to a better place for a young man like you to socialize."

Harold turned down Albert Street and stopped in front of a building just beside the church. "This is the Church Institute," he said. "Inside there's a large hall, stage, and a kitchen. There's always a dance at the weekend. Anyone in uniform can go in and get a nice cup of tea."

Richard hopped down from the cart. "Thank you," he said. "I'll do that. And thanks for the ride."

Harold pointed to the street ahead. "That's Upper," he said, "follow it across to the main road. If I see you on my way back, I'll give you a lift into camp."

The small hand-printed sign on the door, told Richard the tearoom wouldn't be open until the afternoon due to lack of sugar. He walked to the stone bridge over the stream that flowed behind the church. Here he watched a silent flotilla of leaves drift across the water.

Two boys in dark green blazers, shorts, knee-high socks, and sturdy shoes marched towards him along the towpath. The smaller one, carrying a wooden rifle, saluted the older one who was wearing a tin hat.

Richard watched this tiny two-man army with amusement.

At the sound of the town clock, they stashed their gear in a bush, grabbed their school satchels and gas masks and ran off.

Richard walked down the bank to the path and followed them to a street of grey flat-roofed houses. To his surprise, the yellow-and-green truck was in one of the drives.

A woman looked out from behind her front window curtain with a worried face.

"I can't tell if I'm in reverse," Swipes yelled out as Richard approached. "It's bad enough they drive on the wrong side of the road. I don't get these gears."

Richard watched Swipes ram the stick shift into place. The motor roared, tires spun, and the truck jerked backwards into the garden. Muddy earth flew about the lawn. The front door of the house flung open and a woman in a floral apron covered her mouth with both hands. Her eyes filled with tears.

"Not to worry, sweetheart," Swipes called out. "I'll take it slow."

He jiggled the gear again and hit the gas. This time the truck completely flattened two tall wooden poles, bringing a line of laundry to the ground.

Richard's eyes bulged. That would have given his mother a heart attack. The woman went inside, slamming the door. The passenger door of the truck opened and Ted vaulted to the ground. He raced around the front of the truck and yanked open the driver's door. "Get out," he commanded in a loud voice.

Swipes dropped to the ground and rushed to the back of the truck. He braced himself against the rear fender as if he alone could prevent the truck from moving back any farther.

Richard watched Ted attempt to jiggle the clutch. For the third time the truck jerked backwards, knocking Swipes sideways, and collapsing the six-foot fence.

Ted jumped out of the cab into the mess of fence planks and muddy clothes. "This truck is a piece of junk," he muttered. Then, seeing Richard standing across the street, he called out. "Hey Fuller, give us a hand."

Richard walked across the road.

"Get into the cab," Ted said. "Swipes will report in. I'll push."

Happy to help, Richard climbed into the cab. He sat for a moment with his hands on the wheel. "I wonder if this is like Vogel's old tractor," he said out the window, as he jiggled the gear. He pushed down on the stiff clutch. It was hard work, the truck being much heavier than the tiny tractor, but he soon forced the cranky gearshift into action. Richard bit his lip, held on to the stick, and let out the gas. The truck lumbered forwards into the road.

"I got it," he called out the window in excitement, but no one answered. Ted and Swipes were nowhere in sight. As the truck lumbered down the lane, the truth dawned on Richard. Ted and Swipes had left him holding the bag.

Richard drove at a snail's pace, looking up each of the alleyways for the two soldiers. Just before he reached the main road, he spotted a man in the rearview mirror. In a shabby cardigan, brown corduroy trousers, and carpet slippers, the man ran behind him waving frantically.

Richard stopped the truck and leaned out the window to see what the man wanted. He noticed the clerical collar at his neck.

"Hey there soldier," the minister called out between pants of breath. "You can't just drive off and leave that mess behind."

"But," Richard protested, "I was just …"

"I've already made an apology on behalf of the army," the minister said, climbing into the cab. His skin drew tight across his high cheekbones as he glared at Richard from behind heavy-rimmed spectacles. He levelled his eyes. "Something you should have done yourself. Drive on," the minister said, waving his hand in front of his face. "Once we get this truck back to the base, you can tell your story to the battery commander."

Richard drove on to the main road, gritting his teeth. *The sergeant major would have to listen to his side of the story … wouldn't he?*

Back at the hut, the usual game of cards was in progress. Seeing Richard, Swipes stood up and tipped his cap.

"He lives," he said with a grin and sat down again.

Richard stepped aside.

The minister and the orderly officer stepped forward.

"You boys have anything to confess?" the minister asked.

CHAPTER 17

The Battle of the Beans

Dear Tommy,

Even though it is only April, it feels like summer. Remind me to tell you about what happened to the village ice rink when I get home. Thanks for getting your Father to send me the newspapers with Superman's Adventures. By the end of the war, I will be able to live the life of a perfect tramp. I can sleep on hard ground with only a blanket and eat with my pocket-knife. Most guys use their bayonets to open their mail. Remember I didn't like to eat carrots? I do now.

Your army pal,
Richard

◆

"About time, too," Ted said when the quartermaster handed each of them a second pair of boots and another suit of battle dress.

"How long have we been wearing these?" Swipes asked, tugging at his sleeve. "Five months?"

Richard hadn't realized how scruffy their boots and uniforms had become until he received his new outfit. His mother would have made him wear his pajamas until she'd sponged off all the stains. He thought about her for a minute, hoping she was all right.

"After you sign for this report to the motor pool," the quartermaster told them.

"What about rifles?" Ted asked.

"Never mind about rifles," the quartermaster bellowed. "Get over to the motor pool."

Ted was to drive one of the dark-green equipment lorries. Jack got a Ford truck. A huge groan came from those in line when they discovered Swipes was to drive an ammunition vehicle.

"He'll blow us all up," Jack whispered.

"Nah," Richard said with a grin. "He'll never get the thing in gear."

"What about you, kid?" Jack asked.

Richard shrugged. "Guess I'm just a passenger." He hadn't found his name.

"Check again," Jack said. "There's another list behind it."

Richard ran his finger down the names on the second paper pinned to the wall. "I don't believe it," he said out loud. "I got a motorcycle!"

"These twenty-five pounders and eighteen pounders are to be used in turn with the Royal Canadian Horse Artillery," the British artillery officer told them.

Richard could only stare at the huge guns on their carriages, barely hearing the information about new drills and route marches.

"The available rifles and gas equipment will also be shared by different groups."

"Shared?" someone from the ranks called out. "How do you share a rifle?"

"Same way you share a gas mask," Ted responded. "Hold your breath."

The officer looked to identify the soldiers making the comments, but all stared ahead.

When Richard got to his first signalling training session, the situation wasn't much better. Other than the few wireless sets, there were a three sets of Morse flags and a couple of heliographs. The only new item was a set of telephones and a ten line telephone exchange box.

"Some kind of modern army this is," Ted complained to the others in their quarters.

"I did some practical work on the camp telephone exchange," Richard said. "Once we got the hang of it, it was simple."

"Well," said Ted. "We could always bash the enemy over the head with the receiver."

"Nah," Swipes said. "Just call them up and tell them not to bother dropping by."

"Yeah," Jack said. "And while you are at it, tell them the food's lousy."

That was the one truth that bothered Richard as well. He would have given anything to have Mr. Black in the camp kitchen. The food was either under-cooked or over-cooked and always greasy.

The next morning the sergeant informed the troops that the only material available for driving practice was under camouflage.

"What does that mean?" Richard whispered to Swipes.

"It means," Swipes said in a voice loud enough for everyone to hear, "we will be driving imaginary vehicles."

In detachments of six, the men arrived at a large set of wooden boxes, labelled X, K, and H in the middle of the field. One block was to be the troop truck, one the ammunition carrier, and the third the gun carrier. Those designated as drivers were to sit on the blocks, move their arms, and squint straight ahead to demonstrate driving. The men standing behind one of the blocks were to bounce up and down as if they too were on the road.

Orders to move "in convoy," "in deployment," and "in formation behind the leader" resulted in the men moving the blocks to reposition themselves.

"Getting a hang of the gears?" Ted called out to Swipes sitting on top of the box.

Something floated up from the bottom of Richard's mind, something Mr. Black once said to him while making deliveries. "You have to watch out for the guy who thinks being in the army is one big joke. He'll get you killed faster than the enemy."

As Richard watched one of the detachments learn the basics of gun instruction using wooden rifles he couldn't help thinking about the two boys at the bridge. The only difference between his equipment and theirs was that the Canadian troops were supposed to hold off an enemy invasion.

———◆———

Jack sat next to Richard one morning. "So," he said. "What do you think we get to play with today?"

"Bullets," Ted said, pushing his plate away from him.

"We're getting live ammo?" Richard asked.

"Taste your breakfast," Ted said. "Those damn navy beans are as hard as bullets."

Richard and Jack lifted a forkful of beans to their lips. Richard swallowed with a grimace, but Jack spat his out.

The growls and mutterings grew as more soldiers pushed their plates away. Someone yelled, "I want to speak to that cook," and the rest took up the cry. "Cook, Cook, Cook," they chanted as they beat the tables with their knives and forks.

The cook appeared in the doorway. Ted lifted his plate and hurled it into his face. More plates sailed through the air, as men heaved up the tables and tossed chairs. Richard and Jack loaded their spoons and catapulted beans at each other, until the orderly officer appeared at the door and demanded that everyone appear on the parade square.

The battery commander moved down the line asking each soldier the same question.

"Did you take part in this affair?"

"Yes sir," Ted said. "Thought we were supposed to fire ammo, not eat it."

He asked Swipes the same question.

"Yes sir," Swipes said. "I was sending those beans back to the navy."

The real surprise was when the sergeants, who ate in a separate hall, also admitted they had taken part in the battle of beans.

"Either we throw this entire battery in jail for disorderly conduct," the commander told them all, "or we look into the matter of getting another cook."

Several of the men smiled.

"But," he continued, giving them the cold eye, "any further display of this kind of nonsense, and meals will be suspended altogether. The German army is on the move again; it's time we took this damn war seriously."

———————◆———————

Dear Mr. and Mrs. Black,

I received your letter a few days ago, thank you. There was a bit of a riot in the mess hall the other day, which I will tell you all about when I get home.

I met a fellow from the *Evening Telegram*, who had reported on the Honeymoon Bridge. Just before he left for Canada he took pictures of our division and left us copies. Here's one for you.

I'm sitting by the telegraph key. The guys in the background are supposed to be sending signals but I was the only real "sig" available so he had the guys in my troop fill in. Jack Gill is supposed to be demonstrating the heliograph. Ted Billington and Charlie McNaughton are using the flags. Charlie is the guy everyone calls "Swipes."

I've signed up for a seven-week course on signal instruction. Only two Canadians are going. Most of the men in the classes are English. Today the Sarge told me I would be doing some dispatch riding as well. Hope the car is running well.

Your war correspondent,
Richard

Richard had debated whether or not to send the picture to his mother but figured it would just end up in his sock drawer. He knew Mr. Black would put it on his mantelpiece.

CHAPTER 18

The Patrol

Dear Amy,

New men fill the barracks. We now live in
tents on the field.

Richard didn't tell Amy that the noise of the plane
engines overhead made the tin roofs of the barracks vibrate,
which was worse than being in a tent during the rain.

I watched my first bomb explode, even
though it was five kilometers away.

Richard stopped writing. The whole thing had seemed
so unreal. He had heard the drone of enemy aircraft above
the camp as everyone had stopped to watch the plane with
the black Maltese cross on its wing pop out of the clouds
sideways. Richard saw it dive at a sharp angle and covered
his ears as the whine of the engine turned into a scream.
At the bottom of the dive, the pilot dropped his bomb. But
it was no bag of flour. The hill exploded and black smoke
tumbled towards the sky.

The tunnel of smoke seemed to be standing straight up in the air when the RAF plane appeared on the horizon. The edges of its wings twinkled. The first plane turned downward and slid into a dive. It spun as it headed to earth with a thin line of brown smoke streaming from its tail. Before it hit ground, the plane exploded into a ball of yellow.

> The spring sun has been shining every day, and now that we are on daylight savings, the evenings are nice and long. It feels like July. The farmers are plowing and the trees are in bud. Every time we get a break we lie down on the grass with the sun on our face.

"So when is this game of invasion supposed to start?" Ted asked, interrupting Richard's thoughts. Holding a beer bottle in his hand, he walked about the tent shirtless, revealing white skin above his elbows.

"Invasion is not a game," Jack replied. "Especially if those planes decide to drop bombs on us."

"Hitler won't invade England until the RAF is no longer a threat to his troops," Swipes said. "He'll have to break the Brits' air force first."

Richard finished his letter in favour of an early night. His morning duty required him to be on the road by five. It was early, but he looked forward to zooming through the countryside with the cool morning breeze on his face.

The next morning he climbed onto the seat of his Norton motorcycle and jiggled the lever for the gas line on the right handlebar. He rose from his seat and drove his foot down hard on the starter pedal. The engine grumbled but didn't start.

"I know it's early, old girl," Richard said, "but it's time to get a move on."

Richard rose again. This time his machine gave a sputtering roar and a cloud of smoke shot from the trembling exhaust pipe. He headed out into the wet grey morning, the roads shiny with rain, smelling the fields through the reek of oil that travelled alongside.

Designed by a senior officer, Richard's patrol took him along the country roads through the hills and dales, past old ruins and over swollen creeks. Richard had to know how to manage the Norton up steep hills, along narrow roads, around sharp turns, and through large puddles. During each patrol he was to stop at specific places and call in from a telephone kiosk. Richard suspected it was just the army's way of ensuring a regular report, stifling the initiative to explore.

No sooner had he left the camp when a small brown animal scuttled across the road in front of him. He swerved to the left and stopped on the side. The animal rolled itself up into a ball.

Richard noticed a young boy racing across a field waving his arms to flag him down. He recognized him as one of the two young lads he had seen drilling up and down the canal.

"I'm glad you stopped," the boy said. He looked down and then took off his jacket. He rolled the brown ball into it and tied the sleeves. "It's perfect for our back garden."

"What is it?"

"A hedgehog," the boy said. "You've never seen a hedge-hog before?"

"They don't have them in Canada," Richard said. "I don't think."

"Well, we used to have them everywhere, but they're getting harder and harder to find." He slung it over his shoulder. "I'll put this one in my back garden where it will be safe." He started into the field and then stopped. "Actually, I wanted to tell you something drifted across the sky at the back of my house last night," the boy said in a serious voice. "My mum said it was probably a loose barrage from London, but those balloons are silver. I was sure it was white. It could be caught in the trees in the woods."

Richard knew about the blimps that hovered in the clouds over the city. During the day they looked like ugly sausages, but at night they floated like whales on a dark sea.

"Get rid of your animal," Richard said. "We'll take a look."

"I'll come back with the rest of my army," the boy called out behind him. Within minutes, he returned with a smaller boy at his side and a dog at their heels. James introduced himself and his young brother Simon.

"Who is your other friend?" Richard asked as they climbed on to the back of the motorcycle. The dog's mottled nose, different coloured eyes, and single dropped ear gave him a comical look. Despite his broken teeth and scars, his eyes looked intelligent.

"This is Billy. He's a Border Collie," James said. "If any-one can find an airplane, he can."

"If it is a barrage balloon we'll have to take it back to the barracks," Richard said.

"And if it is a parachute," James told Simon, "we'll have to capture the pilot."

Richard smiled at the older boy's enthusiasm as they climbed onto the flat metal passenger seat. "Don't try to lean on the curves," he shouted over the roar of the engine.

Billy ran, tail tucked between his legs, beside the little cloud of steam that came from the motorcycle exhaust. They rode over rocks and roots to the tops of a small forest sitting at the bottom of a hillside. The boys got off. Richard worked his way down the incline, steadying himself with a foot on the ground as he skidded over the pine needle carpet.

Something moved at the far end of the tree line. Richard dismounted and swept his field glasses across the woods. He tightened the focus until he could see the bark of the trees and the leafy branches. A family of deer grazed at the edge of the woods.

"What do you see?" James asked.

"Just deer," Richard replied. *Something must have chased them out of the woods.*

They followed the little-used trail where the earth showed signs of a wide scrape.

The Border Collie tore into the trees.

"Keep an eye out," Richard said as they followed the trail.

The dog stood barking in front of a stand of broken trees. No one was more surprised than Richard when he saw the yellow nose of a crashed plane with German crosses on its wings.

"Did either of you see it come down?" Richard asked.

"We heard aircraft last night," Simon said, "and went out to watch."

"A Hurricane went by," James explained. "We saw a ball of fire going sideways and then one shooting up into the sky. Then we saw the Hurricane do a victory roll."

"Mum made us go back inside because Billy was barking so much," Simon said. "He hates planes."

Billy cocked his leg and directed a steady stream of yellow on to the wreckage as if to prove them right.

"Later, when I went out to use the nessy, I saw the chute float by," James added.

Not far from the crash, a tangle of material in a tree jerked about in the wind. Richard crawled along the branch of the oak on his belly and gave it a tug. As soon as he touched it, he knew it was parachute silk.

"Aren't you going to get it down?" Simon asked when Richard returned to the ground.

"What's the closest building around here?" Richard asked.

"Hill Top Farm is behind these woods," James said. "I'll show you."

Richard peered at the acres of hops that led up to the stone farm house. The rows were tall enough for someone to walk along without being seen.

He adjusted his field glasses and focused on the farmer's face as he chatted to his wife. Richard watched the farmer add a wide length board to the left side of his wagon and a matching board to the other side. He looped the reins over the wagon seat, took his place next to his wife, and gave the reins a shake. The horses turned down the lane.

Everything looked normal, but Richard decided to check it out anyway.

"Are you going up to the farm?" James asked.

"First I'll telephone it in," Richard said. "Then, I'll take you boys home."

"Why can't we stay?" James asked. "We showed you where it was."

"Your mother will be worried," Richard said. "And it's past time for school."

The farm road was full of potholes; some still had water from the morning rain. At the closed gate Richard dismounted and lifted the wooden latch. He tucked the bike behind a hawthorn hedge, removed his goggles, and hung them over the handlebars. He placed his field glasses in his pouch, his helmet on the seat, and his gauntlets inside the helmet.

At the doorway of the dark barn, Richard heard a furtive scuttle. *Could be mice*, he thought, until he caught a whiff of cigarette smoke. *No farmer in his right mind would smoke in a barn full of hay.*

He stepped further into the barn and saw the flash of a match. It flew into an arc, landing in the largest pile of hay.

Richard raced to the spot. Fortunately the match had died out and the hay did not catch on fire. As he bent to retrieve the match, he heard the stuttering whine of his motorcycle. Richard raced to the gate just in time to see its taillight going down the lane.

With a heavy heart he followed on foot, kicking at the stones along the country road. What on earth was he going to tell his sergeant?

Rounding the bend, Richard spotted James and Simon sitting by the side of the road with their heads in their hands. Hearing his footfalls, James looked up, his face streaked with tears.

"Simon," he yelled as he jumped to his feet. "It wasn't him, look, it wasn't him."

"I thought I took you two home," Richard said. "It wasn't who?"

"It wasn't you that went over the edge," James said, grabbing him by the arm. "Come and see for yourself. It's a good thing you can look down at yourself."

Richard allowed the boys to drag him over the rough ground at the side of the road and across the boggy marshland. "Where are we going?"

"To see your bike," James answered.

"My bike," Richard repeated, his face brightening. "Are you sure it's mine?"

His face faded at the sight of the unmoving body of a man sprawled across the rocks at the bottom of the gorge. Richard's motor bike lay on top. His field glasses lay half way down the cliff.

"When we saw you take that path off the main road, we was wondering what you were doing." James said.

"But, it wasn't him," Simon pointed out in exasperation.

"No one uses the scramble path after a rain," James continued. "The rocks get slippery. That's why the bike catapulted into the gorge."

"He was a Nazi," James said with venom. "And he got what was coming to him."

This is exactly what my mother expects to happen to me, Richard thought as he stared down at the broken body. *No wonder she didn't want me to join the army.*

Richard led the boys away from the cliff to the roadway. "Remember," he told them, "that man had a family and they will be sorry for his death."

134

When the squad of armed Canadian soldiers arrived, the sergeant in command immediately ordered the two boys sharing a chocolate bar away from the site.

CHAPTER 19

Recruits

The severe figure of Major McNaughton, followed by two other officers, moved towards Richard from across the square. McNaughton made an impressive soldier in his immaculate uniform and supple, glistening boots. This middle-aged, well-spoken man smelled of pipe tobacco and cologne. Out of uniform, Richard imagined he wore expensive tweed jackets with leather patches on the elbows.

"Bombardier Fuller?" the major asked, standing rigid in front of him. The look on his face told Richard things were more than serious.

"Hold your head up, look an officer straight in the eye, and state your position," the voice of Mr. Black said in his head.

"Yes sir," Richard said, giving his best salute. He focused on the laurel wreath of the major's regimental cap badge.

"That was your motorcycle brought in for repairs?" the major asked.

"Yes sir," Richard replied, staring straight into the officer's dark brown eyes. Deep down in his boots he hoped the damage was only minor.

"No bumps and bruises on your part?" the major asked.

"No sir," Richard replied. His answer held a tiny bit of question to it. Surely the major had received his report, explaining how the bike had gone over the cliff.

"What made you inspect the barn?"

"A pilot would look for a place to sleep away the day," Richard replied. "The best time to travel on foot would be at night."

"Until you provided him with your motorbike," the major responded.

Richard knew he dare not lower his eyes, even though he felt himself going pale. "Yes sir," he responded in a weaker voice. He guessed he was about to be told the bike repairs would come out of his pay. He drew his breath waiting for a lecture on breach of regulations.

"If you had not been so vigilant," McNaughton said, "and had not taken action to investigate, that German pilot could have done serious harm to the farmer and his family. He could also be on the loose making reports to the Nazis." The major turned to the officers at his side. "This is why we will win this blasted war," he said. "Their pilots might be able to fly but they can't drive worth beans."

The officers laughed. Richard wanted to, but knew he couldn't.

"I wanted to tell you I am delighted at the outcome," the major said. "Keep up the good work, Lance Bombardier. When your bike is ready, we'll put you on permanent dispatch."

"Thank you, sir," Richard replied. The major had just promoted him.

In relief, he gave a slight turn of his head, just in time to catch the scowling eyes of Ted Billington.

———◆———

Richard found the two boys parading up and down the street of small houses near the river. Simon followed James, pushing an old baby carriage painted khaki and covered in military insignias. In front of one of the houses a woman swept the path.

Richard got off his bike, saluted them both, and looked in the carriage. He picked out one of the empty Sweet Caporal cigarette packets and frowned. "You're not smoking are you?"

"No, sir," James said. "We keep them for the aircraft identification pictures on the back."

Richard tousled the boy's hair. "I'll make sure you get a few more from the men before we leave," he said with a smile.

"Are you heading to Germany?" Simon asked with wide eyes.

"Just more training," Richard replied. He reached inside his battledress jacket. "On behalf of the Canadian Army," Richard said, "I am to present each of you with a regulation forage cap." Richard had also put a pack of chewing gum inside each cap. "I haven't got anything for Billy, but I will find him something suitable later." He lifted a leg over his bike. "I expect a salute, me being the senior officer of this army."

"Yes sir," both boys chorused. They stuffed their gum into their pockets, put on their hats, and gave him their best salute.

"I've also got a special assignment," he said, beckoning them closer. "Top secret."

The boys huddled around.

"There are rumours that dignitaries will be coming to visit."

The boys snapped to attention with bright eyes.

"I need you two right at the front of the lines, for any possible attempt on their lives."

The boys nodded with furrowed brows.

The woman in front of the house a few doors down stopped sweeping and leaned on her broom. "Are you the same soldier who drove the truck out of my sister's back garden?"

Richard looked up in surprise. "But I ..." he stuttered.

"My boys haven't stopped talking about you since they came home," she said with a laugh. "I'm Carole Hunter," she said, wiping her hands on her apron. "Come in for a cuppa."

As Richard stepped onto a multi-coloured rag rug covering the linoleum floor, Billy came in from the kitchen. The dog paused by Richard's knee for a moment and then lay down in front of him, curled up with his snout resting on his haunches.

"I'm very sorry about the damage done to your sister's garden," Richard said.

"Don't give it another thought," she said, indicating he was to sit. Crocheted doilies covered the backs of all the sitting room chairs. "You drove the truck out, not in. Billy has probably done more damage to the gardens around here than that army truck."

"Dig a lot, do you?" Richard asked the dog.

The dog lifted his head, studied Richard's face for a moment, and then put it down again.

"Nope," James said, sitting on the floor beside the collie. "He chases airplanes, knocking anyone and anything out of the way."

"He doesn't bother with cars but he makes sure those planes head right back out to sea, don't you Billy?" Simon said, rubbing the dog's neck with affection. "Billy can sense them before anyone else can even hear them."

"Most people do not appreciate Billy's efforts at preventing an invasion," Mrs. Hunter said on her way into the kitchen.

"He goes after our planes as well," Simon said. "Billy has sent many women's shopping baskets flying."

"And sent people on bicycles flying," James added. "Mr. Harrison fell in a heap of horse manure," he reminded his brother with a giggle.

"Billy is better than any old air raid siren," Simon said.

"That's why I figured the plane circled back, without its engine," James said. "Billy's nose kept pointing at the ceiling and he barked like mad."

"Why does he do it?" Richard asked.

"He thinks he's working," Mrs. Hunter said, returning with two mugs of tea and a plate of biscuits.

"Working?" Richard repeated.

"He belongs to my uncle, but when he went off to war, we took Billy until he comes home," James explained. "He's used to herding sheep, so he tries to herd the airplanes instead."

"I suppose I could write the German Air Force," the boys' mother said with a wry smile. "I could ask them to stop directing flights over our village."

"Call the British Ministry of Aviation," Richard suggested, enjoying the puzzled looks on the faces of two boys, not understanding the humour of their joke.

"Border Collies are happiest with a job," Mrs. Hunter said, handing Richard one of the steaming cups. "It's sad business trying to keep him inside."

"You can't just tie him up?" Richard asked, picking up a biscuit from the plate.

"We've tried tying him to the tree, but he breaks free," James explained. He fed the dog a small piece of his biscuit.

Mrs. Hunter shot him a glance of disapproval. "And we don't want to tie him so tight he'd strangle."

"Billy is so smart," Simon said. "Billy," he said to the dog. "Introduce yourself."

The collie jumped up, trotted forward, and did a bow. Simon waved his hand and the dog dropped to the floor. The boy turned his hand palm up and the dog rolled on his back, put his paws in the air and froze.

"Ask him if he's dead," Simon whispered.

"Are you dead, Billy?" Richard asked with a wide grin.

The dog lifted his head and gave a long low howl that sounded like, "Nooooo."

Richard laughed. He patted his knee. "Come here boy," he said. But the dog did not respond.

James covered his mouth and blew into his hand. The dog jumped up, walked to the front of the hearth and lay down. James removed the wedge-shaped mouth whistle from his hand and handed it to Richard.

"Have you had to pay anyone for damages?" Richard asked as he examined the whistle.

"Not yet," she said with a shake of her head, "but I can see it coming."

"Does everyone have a clothesline in their backyard?" Richard asked.

Mrs. Hunter nodded.

Richard had an idea. The longer Billy's run, the less damage he'd do, but first he'd talk to Jack and Swipes. Ted, Richard knew, wouldn't bother.

With the addition of a few poles, Richard, Swipes, and Jack were able to hook up a separate line with a lead that ran the full distance of all the backyards. Billy could now run back and forth, chasing his plane and saving them all from attack.

———◆———

Dear Amy,

I had a ringside seat the other night at a large air battle. It seemed like thousands of planes overhead, but who could count, they were moving so fast and in all directions. Planes, both ours and theirs, were falling all over the place. Some crashed and exploded. Other planes flew away trailing smoke. The officers warned us to take cover, because of spent shell cases falling, but we all thought it was more fun to sit on the edge of the trench and watch. The Hurricanes shot down more enemy aircraft than all other defences combined.

> The other day I met a dog that thinks
> he is protecting his family by chasing air-
> planes. I would love to get a dog like that
> when I get home.
>
> I thought you would enjoy this news-
> paper article. You can take it to the Ladies'
> Auxiliary.

Richard folded the small column Mrs. Hunter had pointed out to him in the evening news and put it inside the envelope. He had marked one of the paragraphs.

> When the Mayor made an appeal for knit
> articles for the men serving the forces,
> everyone dug out their needles. Ninety-
> year-old Hilda Arnold saw an opportu-
> nity of doing her bit in a quiet way and
> applied for wool. So far she has knitted
> sixty-five pairs of socks, seven scarves,
> five pullovers, and filled a special request
> for sea boot stockings. Both her sons
> served in the last World War and are now
> with the Home Guard.

What Richard didn't say was they were on their way to relieve the 8th Army Field Regiment at Banstead Park. Not far from Croydon, they would concentrate on firing practice at the Larkhill Artillery Ranges, home to the Royal School of Artillery and the twenty-five-pounder field gun.

CHAPTER 20

The Rabbits of Stonehenge

Dear Richard,

Tommy took your letter to school. He has been writing you the same letter since you went overseas but keeps rubbing out and changing it.

I knitted two more pairs of socks and sent them last week. Mr. Black says that the quartermaster might be giving other people your socks if the parcel doesn't have the right address, but my letters get to you. I even write the word SOCKS on top so no one will think I am a spy.

When you save daylight where does it go? My father always says the point of saving is to earn interest. Does that make the days more interesting?

I hope you are making more money than a quartermaster.

Amy

———◆———

The days of May brought orders of spit and polish for a special inspection.

"Who do you think it's going to be?" Richard asked as he worked at shining his buttons.

"Could be General Gamelin," Jack said. "He's a bigwig in the French army."

"Or Old Ironsides," Ted said.

Soon the news of King George's visit was on everybody's lips. The people of the village talked nonstop about finding suitable positions for viewing. Richard read the posted duty sheet, delighted to learn he was to link up with the King's entourage after his early morning patrol and escort them into camp.

"Take your mother to the knoll just outside the barracks for your security watch," Richard told James and Simon that morning after his patrol. "I'll expect a salute as I pass."

The day of the visit, the newspaper entourage established themselves in their pre-arranged places. Richard parked his bike in the middle of the village crossroads to stop traffic. Everyone chattered and talked as they waited for the royals.

Richard joined the motorcycles in front of the car to lead them into camp, just as a flashbulb popped in his face. He couldn't wink at the boys because of his owl-like goggles, but he nodded. At the sound of the cheers behind him, Richard knew they had seen the King's car. The regiments waited for inspection on three sides of the parade square along with their two new twenty-five-pounder field guns.

Queen Elizabeth greeted the troops in a plain cloth coat, wool gloves, and a jaunty hat that looked like a squashed plate. King George wore an army commander cap. Richard envied his fur collared coat and soft leather gloves.

The band played as they inspected the line. Richard's chest stirred and he held his head high. King George gave a speech with long pauses between his words and the gunners gave three lusty cheers for their colonel-in-chief.

Richard overheard some of the newspaper men's comments as they broke rank.

"Their drill showed a little roughness," one said.

"They've not been mobilized for very long."

"They look like a clean-cut bunch of guys," another said in an American accent.

———◆———

The day after the inspection, the regiment proceeded in convoy to the Salisbury Plains. No one would have believed it was an army on the move with its strange collection of furniture vans, delivery trucks, and buses. The men went into tents across from the ancient Stonehenge ruins. Soldiers sweltering in wool uniforms filled the air with the smell of tobacco and loud stories. Once settled, they stood about their small fires in various states of undress. Cans of tea brewed. Shirts and socks hung on makeshift lines. Then blackout came into effect, fires extinguished, lamps out, and headlights off.

Richard and Jack sat on the brow of the hill that separated them from the stone circle of Stonehenge, listening to the small scuffling sounds in the grass around them.

The moonlight revealed the slopes of the small hills surrounding the stones to be honeycombed with burrows. There were rabbits everywhere.

Richard had the eerie sensation they had moved back in time to what it was like hundreds of years ago when the stones were raised. During the day, they looked like ordinary stones, the kind you'd find in the Niagara gorge. But after dark, they seemed to take on a mysterious faint glow from the moon.

"What are those huge stones?" he asked.

"Something to do with Druids," Jack said with a shrug.

"What's a Druid?"

"People that dance about in the moonlight," Jack said as he headed off to his tent.

Richard looked up at the battalions of stars that revealed themselves in the night sky. The total blackness didn't bother him. He didn't miss traffic signals, or the neon signs of Niagara Falls. His home town was nothing but noise, movement, and excitement. Richard thought about the quietness of the farms along the Niagara River until the hardness of the ground on his bottom made him get up. He left wondering if the stones would still be standing after the war.

———◆———

Fargo camp was a collection of bell tents that held six to eight men. At the end of each battery's tent line, the civilian drivers lived in a huge marquee. It reminded Richard of the circus tent that appeared at home on Stamford Green every July.

The drivers thought working for the Canadians was a lark; paid to drive by day, playing poker, dice, and any other game they could bet money on by night. Swipes and Ted were forever sneaking to the ends of the lines to get into a game.

Richard's evening entertainment was visiting the stones. The rabbits left their burrows and crossed the plain like drops of brown ink. Once Richard watched an eagle wing low, as rigid as a fighter plane. The rabbits darted but one didn't get away from the sharp talons. He heard it scream as it went into the air.

———◆———

Dear Tommy,

Straight across the road from our tents there are some very strange stones. They have been standing up the same way in a circle for centuries. During the day the stones are quiet, but at night they swarm with thousands of rabbits. There are so many it looks as if the ground is moving. I don't know how they survive because there is hardly any grass or leaves left around our huge town of tents and machinery.

When I go over at night the rabbits scatter, but then they come back. I am practicing moving so they won't notice.

There is a new army scheme start-ing next week. I chose mathematics and mechanical arts courses for a start. I'll be able to get a credit to make up for the school I left behind.

Here's a joke for you to tell your friends. Why is it that whenever Mussolini goes to the movies, he always sits in a front row seat? Because it is the only way he's sure to have the Italians behind him.

Your army pal,
Richard

———◆———

Richard spent most of his time laying telephone lines to the pill box observation posts along the coast. As a signaller he had to know exactly where the lines travelled and how to fix them.

"Break in the line," a gunner from headquarters called into his tent as he parted the tent's canvas door. The open flap let in the sharp scent of wet grass.

"It figures," Richard replied with wind howling in his ears. As the storm intensified it would become a blustery wet night. "Who's driving maintenance?" he asked as he buttoned up.

"Billington's waiting," the soldier told him. "Glad it's you and not me."

The windows of the truck fogged up as sheets of rain smeared the road over the downs. Ted flung the truck around curves, lurching one way and the other. He worked the clutch wheels and brakes heedless of their sound. Richard hung on as each thumping bounce threatened to catapult him out of his seat. The truck finally skidded in the saturated ground and fishtailed to a stop. Ted settled behind the wheel and pulled his cap down over his eyes. "Wake me when you're done," he said with a smirk.

As Richard stepped from the cab, the nearby bushes rustled. Something Mr. Black said to him at the train station floated to mind. *"Step carefully and always swing a long stick."* Richard remembered Amy's peal of laughter at his strange advice, but the sounds of rustling bushes made him decide to follow it.

He cut a short, stout branch from a tree. Richard hung his black-out light at the end of the branch and swung it from side to side as he walked. Everywhere there were rabbits. Once he found the break in the line, Richard repaired it. He waited beneath a small bridge for a moment to get out of the driving rain. When the moon came out from behind the clouds, the river beside the road glistened. Richard watched hundreds of wild rabbits nibble the grass along the banks.

From the radio set in the bed of the truck, he called the next outpost. They confirmed his message; the line was good. He could now get out of the rain and back under his blankets. Richard stepped into the cab and shivered.

"Got just the thing for you," Ted said, handing him a silver bottle that looked as if it had been flattened by a train. "Take a swig, it'll warm you up."

Richard lifted it to his lips and took a cautious sip.

"Drink like a man," Ted said with a growl and tipped the flask up from the bottom.

The fiery medicine-like liquid raced down Richard's throat and landed in his stomach like a bomb. He coughed and choked as Ted took back the flask.

Ted tipped it up, swallowed with a gulp, and wiped his mouth with the back of his hand. "I've watched you take lessons in everything the army has to offer," he said with a wicked grin, "except drinking." Ted offered the flask again.

"No," Richard stammered. "No thanks." He rolled down the window for some cool air. Whatever was in that flask, it seemed to warm the entire cab. "You should have seen all the rabbits," Richard commented. "There must be thousands."

Ted pulled up from his slouched position and pushed open the door. From the back of the truck he pulled out a roll of canvas. Richard jumped out to see what he was doing. Ted unrolled the canvas and reached for the sector's Bren gun. He unbuttoned his battledress jacket and placed the automatic weapon into the sling across his chest.

A lump formed in Richard's stomach. "You're going to shoot them?" he asked. "Why?"

"Don't need a reason to kill vermin," Ted replied as Richard skidded and scrambled behind him in the dark. "Good chance for a bit of target practice." He aimed the gun and fired off a magazine along the bank.

Richard's ears filled with the tumult of squealing sounds. When the clouds in front of the moon passed, he looked on in horror at the panting bodies of matted fur oozing blood from backs, thighs, and heads. His nose filled with the smell of blood, making his stomach lurch. He staggered sideways and vomited into the grass.

"Looks like you could use some more Canadian courage," Ted said, reaching inside his breast pocket. "What'll you do when we face the Krauts?"

Richard just waved him away.

He tried to keep his stomach in check on the way back. Every time the truck lurched around a corner, the world went for a little spin.

That night Richard tossed and turned on his cot, not able to make sense of the useless massacre. He tried to calm his mind by remembering the smell of pastry and burnt sugar tarts from Mr. Black's bakery. He thought of his mother's ice box and how you had to keep a close eye on the drip tray. He thought about cutting the front lawn and using the bamboo rake.

When the sun finally rose, it shone right through the first hole in Richard's infatuation with army life.

CHAPTER 21

McNaughton's Flying Circus

Dear Mr. and Mrs. Black

I met a guy I hadn't seen in a long time. Vince Butler, who everyone calls Ape, was with me at Camp Niagara. No one understands why he keeps on calling me Chester. He told me Albert Kennedy, another guy from Camp Niagara, is home. He had something the matter with his eyes.

I was good enough to pass the tests set by the gunnery instructors. Rumour has it the Germans have got better, faster tanks. I hope Superman is keeping an eye on things.

Your war correspondent,
Richard

He wanted to tell Mr. Black all about the weapons he was learning to use, but the army officials warned against it. One weapon looked like a giant piece of plumbing pipe.

They learned how to put a bomb in from the mouth end and let it slide into place. When he held it perpendicular and pressed a button, the bomb shot out, crashing down, one hoped, on the enemy position. The hand grenade was like a metal baseball that had to be thrown in a big arc. When it landed, it blew up, sending an eruption of earth into the sky.

Richard didn't dare tell anyone he was afraid of the sector's submachine gun with the half moon ammunition magazine. He didn't mind his standard British-issue revolver, however. He wore it in a shaped pouch at his waist, like a cowboy with a holster.

Every now and again Richard had to drive the Bren gun carrier, but wasn't happy with the brakes. Once he jammed them hard and the soldier sitting in the back shot out of the carrier. The man wasn't injured, but it gave Richard a shock to turn around and find him gone.

As they prepared to return to Leipzig Barracks, they heard that the German army had invaded Holland.

"France as well," Ted said, throwing his gear onto the van. "You mark my words."

Richard could only think of Mr. Vogel's family.

Richard was promoted to the rank of sergeant. "Your deferred pay," the paymaster told him, "is increased to twenty-five dollars a month. It's all in your book."

New orders came. The Canadian troops were moving into billets at Addington near the city of Croydon, just south of London.

"Divisional headquarters are going to be in Redhill," Swipes told them at breakfast. "The other units of artillery will be scattered about the same area." He took a drink of tea.

"As I figure it," Ted said, "fighting troops have to have easy access to the roads leading to the south coast. That's where invasion troops will land."

"And we are the fighting troops," Richard murmured.

"Fighting troops in civilian houses," Jack said, as he joined them with a notice in his hand. "We'll be at this address for the next fourteen months."

"You got to be kidding," Richard said looking at the paper. "Featherbed Lane?

◆

"It is time to get down to serious business," Major McNaughton barked out the next morning. "We are to train for any task we might be called upon to carry out. Dismissed."

Richard shivered in the late morning air. Riding dispatch had not been all he thought it would be. The weather in this country was not predictable. In a matter of minutes a mass of black clouds would obliterate the beautiful blue morning sky. Huge drops of rain lashed down and the road would be awash with brown rivulets. Even though he had rain gear, the water bounced off his helmet and down his neck. It splashed into his boots and was forever battering his face. The eighteen-pounders were on wooden carriers that seemed to have come from a museum. Machine guns were from the First World War. Personal weapons were still in short supply.

Dear Mr. and Mrs. Black,

The entire British Isles seems to be one big target for enemy bombers, by day as well as night. We have all been on anti-invasion schemes over several days. The whole Canadian army spends time trying to move somewhere or other, take up position, attack, and withdraw. Each exercise has a code name. Swipes says he thinks it is just to fool all the German spies that are running about Britain with wireless sets strapped on their backs.

I receive the odd bundle of papers every once in a while, thanks to Mr. McLaughlin. No one has to look for my name on them because someone on mail duty got so tired of me asking for my socks from home they tie an old one around it. The guys think it is a great joke.

Signal school came to an end. I now wear my crossed flags ABOVE my stripes. I guess I don't have to tell you what it means, but I will. I'm a qualified signal instructor. WHOOPEE!!

Several men left our regiment. Some went home for discharge because they were not fit for further active service. A whole bunch transferred to the

Canadian Provost Corps. We got our first batch of reinforcements everyone calls "Meatheads," because they are actually Royal Canadian Mounted Police, and wear their RCMP cap badge as well as their shoulder title.

Most of the new guys are from St. Catharines. We gave them a warm welcome, not only because we need them, but because they are fresh from home and can bring us up to date.

Tell Mrs. Black thanks for the box of maple sugar. I hope she got the parcel I mailed to her from Plumstead. I thought she'd like to taste some of that chutney stuff.

Your war correspondent,
Richard

P.S. Next time you see my mother please say hello.

What he didn't tell Mrs. Black was the box of maple sugar was crumbs by the time it got to him, but it lasted longer eating it that way. He also left out the part when their British instructor described their first exercise, called Fox, as a "right screw-up." It was supposed to be an anti-invasion exercise in moving the entire division to a concentration area, and then advancing against a hostile force. It began in the early morning hours, and by noon every road in the area was hopelessly jammed with vehicles and guns. When the major general arrived at a crossroads, he found his division approaching from all directions. The signallers had to take over traffic control and order everyone back to their tents without completing the exercise.

For exercise Cat, things went more smoothly, in spite of the wet and muddy conditions.

Bulldog in June took place at night. They camouflaged the equipment during the daylight hours and ended with a mock street fight, eight kilometers from where they'd started.

———◆———

Richard had been riding his Norton motorcycle since they'd left billets that morning. He was not only tired, but once again drenched by a sudden rain storm.

At one of the many halts on the way to the rendezvous area, Jack leaned out of the back of the truck that Ted was driving. "Do you want me to spell you on the bike?"

Richard climbed into Jack's seat in the quad and before he knew it, he'd drifted off.

"Thud," went one of the wheels, throwing him on to the floor of the vehicle. There was a boom and a shudder. For a few seconds there was silence as they all shared the same thought. A bomb!

The roar of the motorcycle brought Richard to his senses. He stuck his head out the back.

"Who the hell is driving this thing?" someone called out.

Ted had just deposited eight tons of artillery in a four-foot ditch.

The main convoy and the division moved past. At the very end of the convoy was the light aid detachment of the Royal Canadian Ordnance Corps. A huge truck with derrick and block and tackle chains swung into position. They hooked chains to the quad and lifted it back onto the road like a toy.

For three hours the stray quad, with Richard following on his Norton, wheeled through traffic to catch up with its battery. Shortly after nightfall they located the other guns a few kilometers from the sea.

———◆———

Dear Amy,

I had been riding my motorbike since we left camp. At one of the halts on the way Jack Gill asked if he could spell me on the bike. Lots of guys offer to spell me when the weather is good, but Jack is the only one who gives me a break from the rain. I took his seat in the quad. Just as I was drying out, we went into a ditch. It scared the heck out of me.

I have an idea about the socks. Don't write the word socks on the parcel. Think of something that no one would want to steal.

Richard

———◆———

The Roft exercise in August was very successful. The traffic control problems had been solved, as they finally had enough Provost Corps people to keep the vehicles running at an even pace, despite the wet muddy conditions. Cascara in August was primarily for the medical services, as they practiced the evacuation of casualties.

Bumper in September was the first time they fired blank ammunition. Richard took the message that their pretend enemy tank occupied the church yard behind the village. They detailed one of the guns to clear the route for advance. It was tricky business, as the streets were narrow. Visibility wasn't more than a hundred feet because of twists in the road, and camouflage covered the spire of the church. The battalion managed to detach one gun from its quad, load it with a blank shell, and push it to a spot off the main street into a side lane. Their plan was to use the gun carrier as bait, to draw the tank out of hiding. The gun would be pushed into the road and blast the tank when it appeared. All gunners hid from view as the carrier rolled along the street. Just as they planned, the tank spotted the front end of the carrier and came out of hiding. Their twenty-five pounder moved into the street and fired.

Every window in town shattered.

TANK DEAD, Richard signalled back, while the officers hid their faces in embarrassment.

◆

Dear Mother,

Things have been busier than I expected, which is why I haven't written earlier.

You once asked me if it would be a privilege to eat off a tin tray. It isn't. I eat sitting on the hard or wet ground, in the back of trucks and sometimes on my motorcycle.

I went to a signal instructors' course. They have the habit of calling us "colonials," so we started to call them "chirpers and limeys." When they complained, the sergeant told them to lay off the colonial stuff and we would be happy to call them anything they wanted.

The course was the usual stuff, and the instructors were very good. Believe it or not, they were still teaching the use of heliographs. They were amazed that I could set up and operate them, while only the instructor and one sergeant from a field battery could do it.

Here, everything stops for tea, no matter where you are or what you are doing. We dig a hole in the ground and fill it with petrol (that's what they call gas over here) and light it. On top of the flames we put a tin can. Everyone adds water from their canteen and Swipes adds the tea. (He always has it on him.) Even though it has bits of wood and sometimes small drops of petrol it tastes good when you've been outside all day crawling around in ditches.

Your son,
Richard

P.S. I hope you are receiving the pay I am sending.

CHAPTER 22

Dick

Richard opened his much-awaited letter from Mr. Black, glad it had come before his leave. The baker's letters never were more than a short note, but Richard knew it wasn't a reflection of his mood. Mr. Black preferred to "chew the fat," his expression for talking, instead of writing. They would have so much to talk about when he got back.

Inside a page of blue, almost transparent, air mail paper were four identical newspaper clippings.

"Hey guys," Richard called as he handed them out. "Looks like we made the paper."

"Which one?" Ted asked.

"The *Toronto Star*."

"It says," Jack read out the headline, "'Gunners Prove Quality in Invasion Manoeuvres.'"

"That has to be us," Swipes said. "They used the word quality." He peered at the clipping and read out loud, "Training month after month over ground where they will fight if invaders land in England, field gunners of the Royal Canadian Artillery have tested and retested battle plans. Proud of their new twenty-five-pounder guns and their gunnery traditions, they have won a reputation in Britain for excellent artillery work."

"Yup," Ted said. "That's definitely us, both quality and excellence."

"Listen to this," Richard said. "The 1st Canadian Division moved to the invasion coast in a three day mock battle against 2nd Division and the British Units. A field regiment from Central Canada and the Maritimes shared in the main attack. After nightfall on the first day, the regiment rolled its guns from the regular gun parks and the convoy sped to a rendezvous twenty miles away where the division collected for the night push."

"They forget to mention that the headquarters for the whole operation was in the local pub," Ted said with a grin.

"In the final quad was the Niagara Peninsula group, Gunner Jack Gill, Gunner Charlie McAllister, and Gunner Ted Billington, all of St. Catharines. They assisted signaller Sergeant Dick Fuller of Niagara Falls, Ont." Richard scratched his head. "Why did he call me Dick?"

"No mention of our accident," Swipes said, "when Ted fell asleep at the wheel."

"The motorized division and several thousand corps troops drummed forward with traffic control soldiers waving hundreds of vehicles along these narrow roads as if it were a four lane highway," Jack said, finishing the article. "Good thing he wasn't around for Fox, eh?"

But Richard didn't answer. He was thinking about this second new name.

"How about coming with me to Oxford," Jack suggested, folding the clipping and putting it in his pocket. "They said they'd welcome any of my army pals."

"I think I'll head to Plumstead," Richard answered. He promised his Uncle Will he'd visit as often as he could. "They'd like to see the clipping."

"Check in at the Beaver Club before you catch your train," Swipes told them.

"That's right," Jack said. "The CBC has a studio there. We can send a message home."

"You've been there, right?" Jack asked Ted.

"Yeah," he said. "But I never mention any names. I just use the word sweetheart and say that she knows who I mean."

———◆———

The studio was nothing more than a battered table and chair at the bottom of a stage. Richard watched the men in uniform sign up at the table and move into line. Some pulled cardboard messages from their breast pockets while others moved their lips in rehearsal. When the chime for the top of the hour rang, the room fell silent.

"Canadian soldiers on leave in London feel right at home at the Beaver Club," the CBC radio announcer said into the thick rectangular microphone perched atop a metal pole. He flicked the switch at the side of the mike. "Ready boys?" he asked and flicked it on again. "We bring you very good wishes as usual from the heart of London, England."

The announcer gestured to the line to move forward as he said, "It is time for us to pay our regular weekly visit to those at home to bring messages and greetings."

The line of men moved to the podium.

"Some of these boys have trains to catch," the announcer said, "so we will hurry them along. Let's start with this rush of Alberta boys."

A cheer rose from the crowd as Jack pulled Richard over to the table.

Army, navy, and air force personnel approached the microphone to tell the listeners at home their name and that all was fine, then thank the family and friends for parcels. Some would claim: "Victory will be ours."

"Where are you boys from?" The man at the table asked Jack and Richard.

"Ontario," Jack replied. "I'm from St. Kitts and my little buddy is from The Falls."

The man at the table looked at Richard. "You old enough to fight?" he asked.

"He's wearing the uniform," Jack said, "isn't he?"

The man shook his head as he wrote down their names. Then he handed each of them a red card. "Go to the front of the line."

Seeing the red card, the announcer signalled for Jack and Richard to move up on stage ahead of the line. "Seems we just had some Ontario boys join us," he said, beckoning them forward. "This is Gunner Jack Gill from St. Catharines, Ontario," he said, reading the card.

Jack cleared his throat and smiled. "I want to say hello to my mother and father on the farm, and my little brother Dave. Let me tell you, Davey, being a farmer is just as important as being a soldier. I'll be home to help you out just as soon as the war is over."

"What would you like to say?" the man asked Richard. The bright stage light and the drift of tobacco smoke made Richard's eyes water. He blinked and said nothing. "Well, Sergeant Dick Fuller of Niagara Falls, honeymoon capital of the world, I might add," the announcer said. "Why don't you say something to the lady that brings these tears to your eyes?"

Richard looked at the mass of men staring at him on the stage. The only thing he could think of to say was, "No socks, so far."

The men in the crowd roared with laughter.

"Way to go kid," the announcer said with a grin. "That was the best message of the night." He handed Richard a pair of tickets to the local cinema, saying, "Courtesy of the CBC."

The men in the club cheered as they left the stage.

Richard handed one of the tickets to Jack and they left waving.

They passed the window of a tattoo shop. Inside a sailor sat with his sleeve rolled up. Richard and Jack stopped to watch the artist prick out a bluebird on the sailor's arm. Seeing them, the sailor lifted his free arm and waved the two of them in with a laugh.

Richard looked at Jack and made a face. The thought of a needle shooting ink into his skin made him wince.

"Wonder if he's getting the guy to write a girl's name?" Jack asked.

"Hope it's a short one," Richard said, "like Amy."

Unlike the movie theatre at home, the tiny London cinema was in a tall, narrow building. The windows in the high ceiling were blacked out to comply with regulations. A restaurant inside served the usual wartime fare of sausages, Spam with chips, or beans on toast. No kids ran up and down the aisles yelling. No crumbled candy wrappers or paper airplanes flew across the seats.

"Wanna grab a bite to eat?" Richard asked.

"We'll go to the chippy down the street after the movie," Jack replied.

"What's the movie about?" Richard asked as the lights dimmed.

Jack shrugged. "Who cares," he said. "It's free."

The show started with a Mighty Mouse cartoon. "Here I come to save the day!" everyone shouted along with the heroic little guy.

When the newsreel started, they watched tanks shooting, bombs dropping, and ships sailing in silence. British soldiers marched prisoners with stiff backs and hands above their heads. "Bloody Jerries," someone yelled.

Then the newsreel showed women working in factories making ammunition, riveting steel girders onto ships. The deep voice of war talked of how peace would come and democracy prevail.

Jack elbowed Richard at the beginning of the main feature. "It's Spencer Tracy," he said with a grin. "Let's loosen our boots."

Halfway into the showing of the feature film, the air raid siren wailed and the house lights went on. The manager went onto the stage. "Everyone must leave for the air raid shelter," he shouted.

CHAPTER 23

Blitzkreig

Debris and stones splattered the wooden doors as the cinema shook around them. Outside, the buses remained in the middle of the road. Dust, smoke, and the smell of burning timber filled the street.

The woman ahead of them complained. "I wanted to stay home and pack up all of my books." She clutched her purse. "If it's my flat that's been hit, at least my books would have been saved."

A man commented, "If you'd stayed home, someone else would be reading your books."

The crowd laughed, making the woman smile as they all headed for the underground shelter.

All summer long there had been tiny specs like mosquitoes circling the skies, but this time it was different. Richard could see a whole phalanx of planes.

Their hum became louder against the drumming of the anti-aircraft cannons. They could hear the thud of explosives coming from the docks. Sprays of sparks danced as the anti-aircraft guns sputtered. Cold fingers of light latticed the skies, illuminating the droning Luftwaffe. A searchlight caught one plane after another and Richard saw the swastika on the wing. His legs trembled and his breath stopped in his chest as they crossed the street.

Richard noticed Jack was not at his side. He turned and called out. "Come on," he said. "We're not far from the underground.

Jack did not answer nor move. He was gripping the iron railing of the downstairs apartment.

Richard shouted again. "Hey, what are you playing at?"

Jack raised his eyes to the sky as the planes dropped their screaming pellets. Enormous columns of smoke rose into the sky. People continued to rush past him, but he didn't seem to notice or care. He couldn't seem to unlock his fingers from the railing.

Richard ran back across the street to him. He put his hand over Jack's tense hands. "It's okay," he said as he unpeeled Jack's fingers one by one. Jack grabbed Richard's arm in a vice-like grip as Richard pulled him into the road.

"It's just over here," Richard said in a low, reassuring voice. But before they could focus on walking, there was a whistle, like that of a freight train, followed by the deafening crash of a high explosion. A shockwave blasted through his body, jerking Richard right out of his boots. His lungs, full of the smell of cordite, hurt.

Jack lay face down on the sidewalk beside him.

Richard scrambled to his feet. He put his hands under Jack's arms and dragged him towards the below-ground staircase.

Another roar made the air around them shudder and Richard's stomach knotted. He tasted vomit in the back of his throat. Then, as if the sky were made of stone, it rained bricks.

———◆———

The sun slipped through the heavy rose patterned curtains of the house in Plumstead. Mrs. Black, in a salmon-pink suit with a broad brimmed hat, white blouse, matching pink shoes, and handbag said, "I'm here for the royal visit."

"How long will the next train be?" Aunt Joyce asked his Uncle Will.

"An engine and five coaches," his uncle answered.

Mrs. Black jammed her fists against her mouth. "He'll miss the train."

"Just you wait while I return," the voice of his uncle came into his head.

"Richard," his mother called out. "It's time for you to come home."

———◆———

Richard felt fingers crawl over his shoulder, raise his arms, and pull at his wrists. Pain shot from his toes right up through his chest. People around him were shouting but he couldn't make out what they were saying. He opened his eyes to see his uniform dark with blood and his left foot dangling like the marionette Tommy kept on his wall in his bedroom. Then he heard the sound of an ambulance. The wreckage of a motorbike came to mind. Someone lay beneath the wheels. *Was it him?*

"Is there flour in my hair?" Richard asked the ambulance attendant.

The man looked at him with raised eyebrows.

173

Mr. Vogel hitched the horse to the wagon. It was Treacle. In spite of being bundled, the cold air chilled him. Richard jumped out of the wagon and puffed to see his breath. He worked several feet ahead of Mr. Vogel, picking as many peaches as he could before the wagon caught up. The horse got a little too far ahead and Mr. Vogel yelled, "Whoa!" The horse stopped. Mr. Vogel said, "You can't get a tractor to do that."

The sounds of squeaking gurney wheels and moans of pain pulled Richard from the warm darkness of dreams. He tried to push away the annoying sounds of voices as he rolled his head side to side across the clean, fresh pillow case. When Richard moved his legs, pain shot up the entire side of his body. One leg felt like it was made of cement. He shivered. His shiver turned into a clammy feeling. His throat was so parched he could have drunk the entire Niagara River. With tremendous effort he forced himself awake into the light. "I'm so thirsty," he said.

Out of nowhere a warm, a soapy cloth went across his gummy eyes and under his neck. A cup came to his lips. He sucked at the water, unable to form a slurp, then fell back onto the pillow, exhausted beyond belief.

Next, Richard woke to the face of an iron watch pinned to the white bib of a dark blue uniform. The woman with soft brown eyes in a hat that looked like it had wings hovered over him. "I've never seen a boy sleep as much as you," she said with a smile.

Richard's hospital gown hung about him like laundry on a line. His bright blond hair was now dingy, his skin pale, and purple circled his eyes.

"Do you think you could manage a piece of toast?" The nurse asked.

Toast! Richard thought. *I could eat a whole loaf of bread. Give me one of Mr. Black's. I'll tear off the crusty top and mine my way through it.*

Richard looked around at the row of men laying in metal cots against green walls the same colour as the Niagara River. "Where am I?" he asked. "I mean I know it's a hospital," he stammered. The smell of disinfectant told him that much, but he had no idea where. He fingered the identification tags that hung around his neck.

"They brought you in a couple of weeks ago," the woman wearing the bib told him. "Your operation was a success, but you've been sleeping ever since."

Richard looked around at the other men in the beds. "Who are they?"

"Airmen," the nurse said. "Most of them have lost arms and legs or are badly burned." She stuck a thermometer under Richard's tongue and picked up his wrist. "Once we get rid of this nasty infection, you'll be up and about. The doctor will be by now that you are awake to explain everything to you."

The sight of the wounded men lying under the grey blankets, unseeing eyes staring across the room, reminded Richard of rabbits. A buzzing sound on the windowsill made him jump. He turned his head to see the large black fly lying on its back on the ledge moving its legs in the air.

The doctor arrived just as the nurse appeared with a plate of toast. He sat on the side of Richard's bed and passed him the plate. "Go ahead," he said. "You must be hungry."

Richard bit into the sparsely buttered slice and chewed as the doctor explained. "I'm afraid I had to remove two of your toes," he said in a low voice.

Richard dropped the toast on the bed.

The doctor picked it up and handed it back to him. "I'm more worried about the infection," he said. "If we can't clear it up with this new penicillin stuff, we may have to take the whole leg. I'm starting treatment tomorrow."

Richard looked down at the tent structure at the foot of his bed. He lifted the sheet. White gauze covered his leg to the knee. Suddenly he remembered the bright flash that had lit up the street and the crumbling wall. Then, the distinct feeling that he ought to be somewhere else flooded his mind. His thoughts clicked into place. "I was heading to Plumstead," he said. "My family is near the Woolwich Arsenal."

"Give me their names," the doctor said, pulling a pen from his pocket.

CHAPTER 24

Kid Soldier

"We need you back on the lines," an officer said to the man in the bed beside Richard.

Richard couldn't help but interrupt. "You can clear me," he said. "I don't use my toes to tap out a message."

The officer came around the bed to inspect the young man sitting in the wheelchair. "Are you a signaller as well?" he asked.

"Yes sir," Richard said giving a salute.

The officer stood in front and scratched his head. "You sure you're ready to travel?"

The nurse overheard the conversation as she entered the room with Richard's Aunt Joyce and Uncle Will. "He is not fit enough to be going anywhere," she said, glaring at the officer.

"We had a free pass to see a London show," Richard told his aunt over the thermometer under his tongue. "We got leave because our regiment was ready to go to the continent."

His Aunt Joyce gave him a weak smile and patted his arm. Richard noticed his uncle showing the officer a telegram.

"And he's made it all the way to sergeant?" the officer asked, with a drop of his jaw.

"I didn't say he was dumb," William said. "I said he was young."

The officer turned to Richard. "What identification did you use when you signed up?"

"My library card," Richard said.

The officer blinked in astonishment. "You won't be old enough until next month."

"Then I'll do new paperwork," Richard said with a shrug.

"You know, you could be court-martialed for this," the officer said, narrowing his eyes.

Aunt Joyce's hands leaped to her face.

"That's okay," Richard said. He stared directly into the officer's eyes. "I've made the papers once already." He passed his spread fingers in front of his face. "I can see the headlines now: 'Kid Soldier Kicked Back to Canada in Cuffs.' My reporter buddies will love it."

The officer grabbed the clipboard from Richard's bed rail. He signed it with an angry flourish, tossed it onto the bed, and marched out of the room.

———◆———

The awful static of the broadcast filled the hospital hall as the voice explained the week's events along with the number of casualties. Richard looked down at his bandaged foot. *Why did the announcer call them causalities?* he wondered. *There's nothing casual about it.*

Richard leaned against his pillow thinking about the

fruit trees, barns, and the great Niagara River. First he was Richard, then Chester, and then Dick. Maybe it was time to get back to being just Richard again.

———◆———

Swipes put his head round the door of the ward. "No one wants you to give up on going to the movies, kid," he said, walking into the room with a large cardboard box. He put the box on Richard's bed and pulled out a home movie projector with a large box of four-inch film spools. The metal projector had a shutter behind a snap gate and a take-up sprocket with a bottom roller.

"There's no belt," Richard said, examining it.

Swipes whipped a stout piece of twine from his pocket and fixed it in place. He cleaned the small lens in front of the battery-run lamp with a breath of hot air and a quick polish with a corner of Richard's bed sheet. He nodded and smiled.

"What are you gonna use for a screen?" Richard asked.

Swipes pulled a flat pillow case up and out of his pants with a grin. He stuck it on the wall of the hospital room with drawing pins and placed the projector on top of the nurse's trolley. He focused the lens with an in-out action and the men in the ward watched Charlie Chaplin and the Keystone Cops to the ticking sound of the turning the handle.

"I was planning to charge all of you guys in the audience a penny," Swipes said with a grin when the lights went on. "That way I'd have enough for a fish supper."

"Play it again and I'll take you myself," the sharp voice of the starched nurse leaning against the wall called out.

The men in the ward responded with shouts and cat-calls.

To create a few laughs, Swipes reversed the direction of the handle.

"Where did you get it?" Richard asked when the lights came on for the second time.

"It was commandeered for a top secret film," Swipes told him. "I thought I'd borrow an extra film and bring it round here before returning it to the cinema." He pulled a chair into the hospital aisle and sat down. "I had to sign for the film and they gave it to me in a sealed container. They even secured the doors with military police during the showing."

Swipes had the attention of everyone in the ward.

"What was the secret film about?" someone shouted out.

"It was some stupid thing about learning how to get in and out of funny-looking square landing crafts," he said loud enough for everyone to hear. Enjoying the audience attention, he stood up. "And get this," he said to them all. "The commentator urged all rifles be kept pointing skyward to prevent injury to the man in front."

The men in the ward roared with laughter.

"And," Swipes said, mimicking the sonorous tone of a broadcaster, "if prone to sea-sickness, avoid disgorging of stomach contents until you reach the shore!"

The second roar of laughter almost lifted the roof.

"So when are we going over?" someone called out.

Swipes tapped the side of his nose and spoke in an affected aristocratic accident, mimicking Lord Haw-Haw. "The day and the hour are the Fuehrer's secret."

"How is Jack?" Richard asked, as Swipes packed up the projector. "I thought he would be in to see me by now."

Swipes looked at the nurse standing beside Richard's bed. The pain on his face was strong as he turned to the projector and fiddled with the reels. "Well," he said with a slight catch in his throat as he looked at the ceiling. "Jack came along with you to the hospital," he said, "but he ended up down the hall, so to speak."

At first Richard didn't understand. He thought about the small walks he took on crutches along the hall. The only thing at the end was the morgue. "Jack's dead?" Richard's eyes grew wide in horror. "And we didn't even make it out of England!"

CHAPTER 25

Socks

"That army buddy of yours certainly has a strange sense of humour," the nurse said, as she handed Richard a shoebox wrapped in brown paper and tied with string.

"What do you mean?" Richard asked. He couldn't get his mind off Jack. It was like having a missing tooth and your tongue keeps going to its empty spot. Every time a soldier stepped into the ward, Richard thought it was him. Just when he thought he had a real-honest-to-goodness friend …

He looked down at the package and recognized the postmark from Niagara Falls.

"It's from Amy," he said with a smile.

"Is she your sweetheart?"

"Just a neighbour," he said. But thinking about her gave him a peculiar kind of ache.

"Take a look at what it says on the sides and back," the nurse said.

Richard flipped the box over. In dark black letters, the words "Dead Canary" filled the back. The same message marched along all four sides of the box as well.

"Amy wouldn't actually send me her dead bird," Richard said as he opened his pen knife. "Even for a scatterbrain like her, this is strange."

He opened the parcel, tossed the paper and twine to the side of his wheelchair, and put his hands on the lid. The thought of a dead animal of any kind brought the bloodbath of rabbits back into his mind. He left the box on his lap and shut his eyes.

"You didn't break the poor girl's heart, did you?" the nurse asked.

"No," Richard said. *If you've got the courage to be a soldier,* he told himself, lifting the lid, *a parcel from home shouldn't be such a scary thing.* A flash of yellow made him close it.

"Well, if it is a dead bird," the nurse said, "I can't have its germs in my ward." She took the box from him, ripped off the lid, and lifted out the soft yellow bundle. An outrageous pair of yellow socks unfolded like Christmas stockings with an orange in each toe. A piece of paper fluttered down.

Richard caught it with a smile.

Dear Richard,

For a quarter we can buy a stamp for a war savings bond. One booklet has sixteen stamps, which comes to $4.00, but guess what? When you cash it in, you get $5.00. Do you think your quartermaster knows about this?

Remember the bird cage in my front window? Yesterday my canary was on his back with his little legs sticking straight up in the air. His feathers were still bright yellow but his eyes were dull.

Tommy dumped the cookie crumbs out of one of mother's tins and I put in a layer of tissue paper. He took the bird from the cage and put him on top of his little white sheets. I stroked his breast before closing the tin. Tommy dug a hole in the backyard and surprised me by cutting one of mother's best roses. I wrote out an ice cream stick cross since I couldn't write on the tin. That's when I had this amazing idea.

Mrs. Black gave me this shoe box.
Watch the birdie!

Amy

A scrawl of different ink filled the bottom of the page.

The newest bomb sights used are "hush-hush" instruments and no one on the inside knows their performance. It is rumored they are positively uncanny and Herr Hitler is in for a rude lesson in accuracy if and when the curtain goes up on the big-time show. E. Black

Richard requested pen and paper from the nurse.

Dear Mr. and Mrs. Black,

On my leave, I went to a place in London near Trafalgar Square where soldiers from Canada could go to relax. At the door there was a barrel full of apples from Ontario and you could help yourself. I ate two, right on the spot. A guy from CBC radio let me send a greeting. Did you hear it?

A stick of bombs dropped while we were in the movies. One bomb sheared off the top floor of the buildings. I picked up a piece of shrapnel as a souvenir.

Your war correspondent,
Richard

He didn't tell them that the piece of shrapnel had caused the infection in his leg, he'd lost a few toes, or that the army had deemed him no longer fit for service.

———◆———

Months later, when his orders finally came through, Richard barely glanced at the pay packet, letter for the bank, and boarding passes for the train and ship home as he stuffed them into his breast pocket. With one swipe of his hand, everything he owned was in his rucksack.

Why? he kept asking himself. *It's only two toes. It wasn't a whole leg.*

"One last letter," the nurse said, handing him a thin blue envelope before she wheeled him to the front door of the hospital. He took it eagerly. It had been four months since he'd heard from Mr. Black. But seeing the writing on the envelope, his heart missed a beat. It was his mother's spidery scrawl. *That's odd*, Richard thought. *She never wrote before*. He held it in his hands for a moment, unsure if he should open it in the corridor. Richard decided to save it for the train and tucked it into his uniform pocket. He shook hands with the nurse and left.

Even though Richard wanted to limp, he took great care to walk upright. The doctor told him the best thing for recovery was walking, but Richard would have done it anyway. He was so used to it being his only way of getting about. Besides, it helped with the restlessness he felt from being so long in the hospital. Along with the loss of his two toes, he had a permanent patch of red welted skin below the knee. He prayed he wouldn't have to use a cane when it got damp.

Richard passed a long row of brick houses, but they weren't houses anymore. The hunk of mortar missing from the end of the row looked as if someone had taken a giant bite. When he turned the corner he faced an endless mass of rubble, brick, smouldering timber, and broken chimney pots. The smell of dust and powdered brickwork still hung in the air.

Across the street, he could see the morning sunlight filtering through the backs of the destroyed houses. Like Amy's old doll house, the entire front wall was gone. Curtains flapped in the breeze, crooked pictures hung on wallpapered walls, and a ceiling light swung in the breeze.

It was the staircases that bothered him most. So many sets of stairs going to open sky.

At the sound of crunching glass, Richard looked at his feet. Millions of fine slivers of glass coated the road.

A woman across the road held her coat over her arms, staring up at the place where she most likely used to live. Gazing at the shrapnel-spattered walls, Richard tried to imagine what it would be like if his home town had been bombed.

Past a small park, the surprising smell of tree sap made him stop and gaze about. The bombs had blasted the bark and leaves from the trees leaving their branches covered with clothes and debris.

Richard waited at the bus stop, watching the red double-decker drive around the huge potholes in the road. Outside the train station, people hauled away bricks in wheelbarrows. He paused to stare at a pair of men's dusty shoes still sitting on display in a broken shop window.

The short blast of the train made him jump.

The rain blurred the view of the dark wet country-side as they travelled in silence.

Richard remembered the letter in his pocket just as the train stopped with a lurch and went into dark-ness. Knowing they would be staying put for the night, Richard stretched out on the floor to ease the ache in his leg. His mother's letter would have to wait until morning.

CHAPTER 26

Home

As the train made its way into the Niagara station, the pre-dawn city lights made Richard feel like he was heading for a circus. At the platform he stopped to breathe in the river air and listen to the roar of the falls. The station master, seeing his uniform, grabbed his hands and pumped them like he had a fish at the end of a pole. Then he pounded him on the back and welcomed him home in a hearty voice.

Richard walked along Queen Street, trying not to limp. He hesitated outside a men's clothing store. He could certainly do with some new clothes as there'd be no chance the ones he left in his closet would still fit. That was if there still was a closet for him to open.

What would he do if another family was living there? He supposed he could go over to Tommy's place. They would know where his mother was.

As he got closer to home, Richard felt an emptiness beneath his ribcage. It was like homesickness, which didn't make sense because he was almost there. Then he knew. It was Mr. Black.

Half way up Maple, he spied the cherry tree. The hedge was in need of a trim. Richard stepped up onto the porch, put his hand on the knob, and turned.

The house was so quiet he could hear the desk clock ticking in the front room. Lowering his rucksack to the floor, he looked into the dining room. All the same furniture with the smell of lemon furniture polish. On a small round table, under the window, the fern in its dimpled brass pot looked wilted. Richard reached for the small green watering can beside it and gave it a drink. Beside it sat a double-hinged frame. He picked it up.

The photograph of his uniformed father jolted him into remembering the loud steady rhythm of his own boots as his troop marched to the St. Catharines train station. Their belts, buckles, and badges gleamed in the sun, as they all stared straight ahead.

The other side of the frame held a photograph taken at the end of the day they had all gone to Niagara-on-the-Lake. There was a touch of flour in Richard's hair. He put the frame down and went into the kitchen. It looked larger without the clothes horse and galvanized buckets.

At the back of the house, where the closed-in porch protected the back door, Richard was surprised to see the long narrow window, where the clothesline came through, shut.

His mother had been so precise about hanging her laundry. She took two corners of a bed sheet out of the basket and folded it in half. Then she placed the clothes pegs at equal distance along the line. Grace hung the pillow cases from the seam so that they would billow in the breeze. All socks had to hang by the toe, in pairs, with heels in the same direction. He smiled. It was as if a random assortment of different sized coloured socks on the line indicated a mad woman lived here. She would have done well in the quartermaster corps.

The handwringer still stood on the floor but the wicker basket beside it was gone. Amy was right. There wasn't a sign of laundry business anywhere.

Richard went out into the backyard. Raspberry canes and currant bushes lined the back fence. The small leaves of carrots and radishes sprouted in a patch. At the side of the house, the bamboo rake rested beside the push mower. He walked around the house to the front.

With great difficulty, Richard climbed the cherry tree. The old railroad lantern was right where they left it, tucked inside the apple crate they used for a table. Richard lifted it. The sloshing sound that came from the base told him it still had oil. He removed the glass flue and turned the coin-sized dial to lengthen the wick. He felt for the small metal tin of matches, struck one, and lit it. The smell brought back memories of tents, bomb shelters, and trips to outhouses. He stretched out on the platform and as he thought about the 1st Canadian Division heading overseas and fell asleep.

When he woke, it was almost dark. Entering the house he heard his mother humming a tune in the kitchen. She placed a brown teapot on a blue and white checker cloth alongside a can of evaporated milk. Her hands were no longer reddened and calloused from the soap and scrubbing board. Her hair was different as well. Cut to the chin, it was dark brown. Instead of her usual flowered housedress, she wore a long-sleeved navy dress with small pleats down the front and a pearl necklace. She looked like she had been somewhere special.

"I told you not to sign up," she said to him in a quiet voice.

"I know," he replied, almost whispering.

"The whole time I waited for a telegram."

Richard said nothing as he sat down.

Grace appraised her tall son with his father's corn silk hair and sky blue eyes. He had grown taller, his chest and shoulders broader. She pulled out a chair, sat down, and pushed the teapot towards him. Richard lifted it, filled her cup, and then his own. She pushed the sugar bowl toward him. He shook his head. He had gone so long without, there was no need.

"You left me all alone," she said, "with nothing but laundry." She made it sound as if all the dirty laundry in the house had been his.

Richard sipped his tea, watching her over the rim. He put the cup down. "When did you lose your job?" he asked.

"Lose my job?" she repeated in astonishment. "I got a better one." She took her tea cup to the sink, rinsed it, and turned it upside down on a folded tea cloth. "Mr. McLaughlin took me on at the bank." She turned to Richard and gave a weak smile. "I should have stopped doing laundry as soon as you went to school."

Grace Fuller picked up the navy hat sitting on the enamel ledge of the counter, removed the long pearl-tipped pin from its brim, and put it back in. Then she moved to Richard and placed her hand at the side of his cheek. "Don't you ever go away like that again," she said to him softly. "You're the only family I've got."

"We've got family in Plumstead," Richard said.

Grace sighed and put down her hat. "Edith wrote," she said as she unpacked the paper grocery bags on the counters. "But you know it's not the same."

That didn't surprise Richard. Edith was the type to write to newspapers, church councils, members of parliament, and probably the prime minister himself.

"You better visit the McLaughlins," Grace advised him. "News travels fast."

"I thought they would have been here by now," he said, trying to keep the disappointment from his voice.

"Tommy won't be by until he finishes up at Vogel's," she said. "And you didn't think Amy would let you see her in anything but a new dress?"

"I've got somewhere to go first," Richard told her. He had promised Mr. Black he would be the first person he'd visit when he got home. Despite the circumstances, he intended to keep that promise.

Richard walked up the street to the bakery. Mrs. Black stood in the front window, pulling on her sweater as if waiting for him. Before he knocked on the door it opened. Her face was thinner, black circles sat above her cheeks, and her skin had lost its lovely pecan shine.

She took Richard by the hand and they headed to the cemetery. His mother's letter had broken the sad news.

Richard had never really known his dad. That's why it was so easy for him to visit his grave. But this was different. Mr. Black was a real person. Beneath the grass, in a row of stones, there was a real man he'd known and admired.

Mrs. Black held a linen handkerchief to her eyes. Richard's throat went dry. "He was such a good man," she sobbed as she leaned against Richard. Richard wanted to say he shouldn't have left, but there was no point. It wouldn't have changed anything. All he could do was stand and stare at the tall granite slab adorned with a sheaf of wheat.

Walking back towards the house, Richard saw the curtained windows of the bakery and the closed sign. He placed his hand on the hood of the black car. "How is she running?"

"You know, I don't understand anything about cars," Mrs. Black said with a small smile. "I've got something for you inside," she told him as she opened the bakery door. The sun streamed through a chink in the curtains, casting a stripe across the dusty wood floor. The aroma of fresh bread had disappeared. Now there was just mustiness.

The two draped squares in the walls drew Richard's attention first. "You don't use the ovens anymore?" he asked.

"It was the rationing," she responded in a quiet way. "Once gasoline, butter, and sugar went, he couldn't operate properly. He shut the bakery and went to work at a plant."

Richard looked at her wide-eyed. "He never told me anything about that."

"Welland Chemical took him on the basis of his military record," she said, leaning against the large dusty baking table. "They made explosives. He didn't like to talk about it."

She lifted Richard's hand, placed the set of car keys into his palm, and closed his fingers around them. "There's plenty of gas in the tank. You can drive it home now. We'll transfer the ownership later."

"I can't take his car," Richard stammered. "You should sell it or something."

"I never argued with him while he was alive," Mrs. Black said, "and I won't now. My husband told me you were to have it." She pointed to the string-tied bundle of letters on the mantelpiece. "He was so proud that you wrote to him."

When Richard entered his own kitchen, a small chicken waited in a roasting pan. He watched his mother move about, setting the dining-room table.

"Mr. Vogel stopped by the bank to ask how you were doing," she said. "He's planning to sell the farm and live with his brother in Toronto."

Richard slumped into his chair. *No farm, no peaches, no bakery, no pies.* The world he had looked so forward to coming back to was gone. He put his head in his hands.

"We're going to the McLaughlin's after dinner," she told him. "Amy's talked the Ladies' Auxiliary into giving you a welcome home party." His mother busied herself mashing potatoes. "I can't stay too late. I've got to be at the bank first thing in the morning."

Richard remembered the paperwork he was to take to the bank. Something lifted in his chest. "I'm going with you in the morning," he said, standing up.

"Why?"

"I'm not old enough to put my name down on a mortgage," he explained.

"For goodness sake, we don't have to mortgage the house!" his mother exclaimed. "I've worked hard to pay the bills," she said with a sniff.

"Oh there will still be plenty of hard work," Richard said ruffling his mother's hair. "I'm going to buy Vogel's farm. The three of us can manage it. We'll do the work, you can keep the books."

"Mr. McLaughlin won't be happy if I quit," she said, wiping her fingers across her eyes and then on her apron.

"You could stay on at the bank if you like it," Richard said.

"I do," she said, with a small twinge of a smile. "But how am I going to get back and forth to work from a farm?" she asked. "There's no bus."

"Women are just as good drivers as men," Richard said. "In London I saw a woman driving a fire engine."

"I don't think I'll need a fire truck," she said with a much larger smile.

"We've got a car!" Richard yelled. He picked his mother up and twirled her around the kitchen. "You can drive yourself to work!"

Author's Note

Most young men, like my father, participated in the Canadian Army Summer camps for excitement and adventure. Details of this story come from my father's diary. Having trained under the assumed name of Chester Lee Huston for one year, he joined up underage.

Canadian Car and Foundry manufactured Hawker Hurricanes between 1938 and 1943. Number 1 Squadron RCAF in the Battle of Britain used Hurricanes to play a decisive role in the Battle of Britain and went on to fly on more fronts than any other British fighter.

The 1st Canadian Division mobilized before the formal declaration of war on September 1, 1939. They crossed the Atlantic in December 1939. Several announcers on the English language propaganda radio program *Germany Calling* gave out false reports of the convoy. Dismissed by many, as comical figures they all went by the nickname Lord Haw-Haw.

Leipzig Barracks on Ewshott Common, now demolished, was originally built for the Royal Field Artillery. The division trained in England for three years before transferring to the Mediterranean to take part in the Invasion of Sicily in July 1943.

The bombing of London started on Saturday, September 7th when 967 German and Italian fighters and bombers attacked at 5 p.m. The main objective was the densely populated East End, Beckton Gas Works, and Woolwich Arsenal. Blitzkrieg was the term used to describe the German armored punch that was fast and furious and totally confounded the enemy. It was a great way to attack either by air or land, but a poor way to defend.

Special thanks goes to Ken Fuller for his technical and military editing and unwavering brotherly support. Thanks also go to Anna Gemza, Marjorie Cripps, Corinne McCorkle, and Angela Collier for marching through the pages alongside me; Brenda Julie, Nancy Wannamaker, and Amy Hurst my avid readers; Sylvia McConnell and Jennifer McKnight at Dundurn; and my always-willing-to-listen husband, Stan.

JENNIFER MARUNO'S CHERRY BLOSSOM BOOKS

When the Cherry Blossoms Fell

9781894917834
$9.95

Nine-year-old Michiko Minagawa bids her father good-bye before her birthday celebration. She doesn't know the government has ordered all Japanese-born men out of the province. Ten days later, her family joins hundreds of Japanese-Canadians on a train to the interior of British Columbia. Even though her aunt Sadie jokes about it, they have truly reached the "Land of No." There are no paved roads, no streetlights, and not streetcars. The house in which they are to live is dirty and drafty. At school Michiko learns the truth of her situation. She must face local prejudice, the worst winter in forty years and her first Christmas without her father.

Cherry Blossom Winter

9781459702110
$9.99

Ten-year-old Michiko wants to be proud of her Japanese heritage but can't be. After the bombing of Pearl Harbor, her family's possessions are confiscated and they are forced into deprivation in a small, insular community. After a former Asahi baseball star becomes her new teacher, baseball fever hits town. Then the government announces that they must move once again. But they can't think of relocating with a new baby coming, even with the offer of free passage to Japan. Michiko pretends to be her mother and writes to get a job for her father on a farm in Ontario. When he is accepted, they again pack their belongings and head to a new life in Ontario.

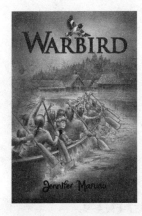

Warbird

9781926607115
$9.95

In 1647, ten-year-old Etienne yearns for a life of adventure far from his family farm in Quebec. He meets an orphan destined to apprentice among the Jesuits at Fort Sainte-Marie. Making the most impulsive decision of his life, Etienne replaces the orphan and paddles off with the voyageurs into the north country. At Sainte-Marie, Etienne must learn to live a life of piety. Meanwhile, he also makes friends with a Huron youth, Tsiko, who teaches him the ways of his people. When the Iroquois attack and destroy the nearby village, Etienne must put his new skills into practice. Will he survive? Will he ever see his family again?